# Not My Type

By
## Autumn Siders

Printed in the United States of America

First Printing, 2020

ISBN 9780578679754

E.M. Sanchez Press
PO Box 82
Moultonborough, NH 03254

www.autumnsiders.com

Cover Art by Kerry Swain and Autumn Siders

Al Sr. Nieve
*Sigue tus sueños*

# Black Rose

*There was a black rose that grew in the forest, and for some reason, this rose never bloomed. It stood in the ground waiting for its chance to open. For a very long time, no one came across this hidden beauty in the darkened forest.*

One day, a family decided to go camping in those very woods, and so they packed their car and set on their way to the wilderness. The Trident family consisted of the mother, the father, and two daughters. The oldest daughter, Gillian was a bit stuck up but very studious. She was against this camping idea all along. The youngest daughter, Martie, was the exact opposite of her sister and thought the idea of roughing it in the woods for a couple days was the greatest thing ever.

As soon as the Tridents arrived at the area they would call home for the next couple days, Martie went off to explore while Gillian found the cleanest stump in the area and sat to touch up her makeup and check her appearance in a compact mirror. The girls' parents quickly set up camp so that all would be prepared by nightfall.

Meanwhile, Martie had strayed a little too far from camp, and although she was sure she could find her way back there was a dark feeling that grew inside her and she could not shake it. The farther Martie strayed from camp, the lower the sun got in the sky.

Despite the strong urge to turn back, Martie had a stronger urge to carry on deeper into the woods. It was almost as if she were being told where to go by her heart. Finally, she reached a clearing in the woods, and in the middle of the forest floor, there stood a solitary black rose.

That very rose had stood there for centuries, but who had planted it or why was unknown. It was obvious this flower held special powers.

Martie, of course, knew none of this, but surely it was odd to find this lonely rose out here in the woods. She went over to the flower, and even though she knew she would regret doing it, she could not stop herself. She plucked the rose from the ground and quickly ran back the way she came.

Luckily, she could hear the voices of her family calling in the distance because as dark as it was, she could barely see her own hand in front of her face. She was going to have to find her way back to camp by the sound of their voices. Just when she thought there was no hope, she heard the crackling of fire and saw a light up in the distance.

As she stumbled out of the trees, she saw scowls on her parents' faces. The flicker of the firelight made them seem even more ominous, but for once she was happy for her parents scolding her; at least she was back in one piece.

After dinner, they all crawled into the tent that was a little too small for them, but they somehow managed to fall asleep. A couple hours after the tent filled with snores, Gillian woke up, startled. She thought that she had heard a growl and was immediately reminded of her haunting childhood dreams of being chased by a bear. It was these visceral memories that made her not want to go camping in the woods.

She was wide awake now, and this time she heard another growl. She quickly rolled over to wake her dad but realized he was not there. In fact, she was the only one in the tent, and her entire family had disappeared. With no one there to console her, she decided the best thing to do would be to pull the blanket over her head and go back to sleep. It had to be another one of her dreams, and when she woke up everything would be fine.

Morning came, and still Gillian was the only one in the tent. She hadn't fallen back to sleep but had kept the blanket pulled over her head and not opened her eyes until she couldn't stand it anymore. When she finally did open them, dawn crept in the tent through the flap that was ajar. Martie was not in her sleeping bag, but something else was: a wilted black rose.

As soon as Gillian realized that last night had not been a dream, she ran out of the tent screaming. After a moment of utter chaos, she discovered that it was not morning. The light she saw in the tent was actually the headlights of their truck. Then she heard shouting from very angry men.

She ran behind some trees and heard a whisper.

"Gillian, it's me."

From behind the tree next to her, Martie appeared. She had never been happier to see the brat in her whole life.

"Where are Mom and Dad?" Gillian asked.

Her sister said nothing.

"Martie, where are Mom and Dad?"

"Let's go."

Gillian had no idea where they were going, but she trusted her adventurous sister and she had nowhere else to go, so she followed.

Martie led the way, and this time she knew it much better. She went straight back to the clearing in the woods, but this time there was a marvelous village filled with gold.

Gillian was in shock. She had no clue what to do so she asked one more time, "Where are Mom and Dad, Martie?"

"They are dead," she replied. "That's the price we had to pay for all of this."

Gillian couldn't speak. Her parents were dead, and she had no clue why.

Worse than that was how calm and practical Martie was. It was like she was in a trance and just going through the motions. "The short story is, I found a rose last night. It was a magical rose. We can have anything we want now, but Mom and Dad had to die."

"I'm going to need more than the short story, Martie. What the hell is happening here?"

"We can have all we ever wanted, Gillian. We don't need Mom and Dad. The rose will grant our every wish." The more she thought about it, Gillian realized she had always been the black sheep of the family anyway. When she was younger, she had dreams that were so real. They were always about things that hadn't happened, but within days, whatever she dreamed about would come to fruition. Her parents never believed her and instead sent her to a therapist. Childhood was not all that great. Was it really all that bad to lose her parents but gain all this wealth? She could buy new parents.

The ease with which she had these thoughts was frightening, but at the same time, she knew Martie was right and that the rose would give them all they needed. The panic that settled in when she'd awoken in the tent had drifted away, and Gillian felt nothing but calm and sure that trusting her sister and the rose was the right decision.

Martie explained the last rule, "We can never take the gold out of the forest, or it will turn into fool's gold. But anything we wish for will come to us."

Gillian knew in her heart what she felt was wrong, but really this was a small price to pay for such extravagance. Overwhelmed by it all, she decided to take a nap on her new bed of gold.

The next morning she awoke in her bed at home to the sound of her mother's voice.

"Gillian, wake up."

As she slowly opened her eyes, she heard her dad shouting from downstairs.

"Hurry, Gillian. We want to make it to the campsite before nightfall. You never know what can happen in those woods at night."

## Colin

### Saturday, August 22 8:12pm

*Ssssurgat…*

I am not sure if I hear that at first.

*Ssssssssurgat…*

I definitely hear it now. It is so quiet, but the hiss of the "s" is hard to miss. I know I locked the door before I came back here to close out for the night. Maybe there was someone still in the aisles that I missed? I quickly lock the cash up in the safe and head back up front to check out what's happening.

"Hello?" I wait for an answer, but all I hear is the humming of the fluorescent lights. I look over at the door, and it is ajar. I may have forgotten to lock it, but there is no way I would leave the door unlatched. I cautiously walk over to it and open it the rest of the way. I peek my head outside and find no one there. I am not normally a jumpy person, but since we played around with the Ouija board last night, I am a little on edge.

I wrangle my keys out of my front pocket, latch the door, and lock it. This time, I check it twice. I may be in a hurry to get out of here, but I don't need to deal with Bill yelling at me tomorrow. I told Aimee that I would come over right after work since I am not the only one on edge after last night's events. My rational brain tells me it was just Alex moving the planchette, but when the lights are dim, the candles are flickering, and your girlfriend is squeezing your hand so hard it cuts off the blood flow, the pointer could be spelling out "puppies" and you would still shit your pants. At least Alex didn't go for anything too scary, just a few random letters. *E. T. T. U.*

I try to clear my mind of that as I head back to the office. I bend down to open the safe, but the door creaks open on its own.

"Come on, what the hell?" I *know* I locked that door. After working at Bill's Hardware for five years, this is a mistake I would not make. All the employees were given the lecture. We had been robbed a few times over the years, and Bill always told us that the money went in the cash register or in the safe and both were to remain locked at all times.

I scoop up the stack of bills I placed in there and quickly count the money and match it up to the sales for the day. It's all there. I sigh in relief. I do not need Bill on my back. This is my last night in this deadbeat town then I'm off to college.

*Knock! Knock!*

I jump. Look at me, afraid of my phone. Maybe I should choose another notification sound. I pick it up and read the text message from Aimee.

*R u done yet?*

B there in 20. u ok?

*Yea. can you hurry tho? I don't want 2b alone*

Just lockin up. b there soon

I put the money in the deposit bag and stick it back in the safe. This time I close the door firmly. After I lock it, I pull on it twice to make sure that it won't be opening again. It is definitely locked. I shut the lights off in the office and make my way back up front. I take a quick look around and make sure that everything is in order and then head over to the light switches. I click them all off and as I am standing in pitch black, I hear it.

*SSSSurgat....*

I immediately flip the lights back on and look around frantically.

"Alex?! If that's you, this is not funny!" I wait for a response but hear nothing. "Alex?" I wait in silence.

*Creeeaaakk*

I watch as the front door slowly opens on its own.

"Fuck this shit! I am outta here." I flick the lights back off and head straight for the now open door. I cannot get outside quickly enough. As soon as I step out of the building, I slam the door shut behind me and jam my key into the lock. The tumblers click as I turn the key and take a deep breath of fresh air. I glance back through the window, expecting to see something moving around inside, but instead I see darkness.

"It's just my imagination." I turn around to head to the car and as soon as I take a step, there's a *whooosh*.

"Watch where you're going!" shouts a man on a bike. His voice fades as he zooms away from me, and the flashing red light on the back of his bike looks like a demonic cyclops winking.

"Get a grip," I tell myself as I realize I am acting like a scared child. I take a few breaths and calm my nerves. This time I look both ways and then step out into the parking lot. I hear the chatter of the crowd up at the pub, and a dog barks in the distance. I am comforted by the sounds of life. I am not alone.

*Knock! Knock!*
It's Aimee.

*Where r u?*

*Have u left yet?*

*On my way. Don't worry*

*Shuffle, shuffle.*
I stop texting and look behind me. There is no one there. I pick up the pace, only a few more steps until I reach the car. The hairs on the back of my neck are standing on end. I fumble with my keys, and when I find the right one, I slide it into the lock. When I turn it, there is no resistance. The door was already unlocked.

"No way!" I am on the verge of screaming like a child as I back away from the vehicle. I always lock my car. I am obsessive about it. I inch closer and look in the back seat. Nothing. I look in the front seat. Nothing. I look in the back seat again and open the door. Nothing.

I just need to get out of here at this point. I climb behind the wheel and quickly lock all four doors. Unless someone else has a key, I am safely locked in the car. I slide my key into the ignition, and the engine comes to life. I shift into reverse and look in the rear-view mirror. Instead of seeing the asphalt of the parking lot behind me, I am looking right into two red eyes, which are looking right back at me.

# Alex

## Saturday, August 22 9:02pm

This is going to be the worst night ever. I just love when other people don't show up for work. Like I didn't have any plans that don't consist of pulling a double tonight?

"These shelves don't stock themselves," Dick chided.

He knew I wouldn't say no to staying since I needed the money, so here I am on the last Saturday before my friends go to college and leave me behind to rot in this backwoods town.

I had some good plans for this evening too. After Aimee and Colin were so freaked out by the Ouija board last night, I fully intended to head over to Aimee's and scare the hell out of both of them. I have to admit, it was a little creepy, but I am sure that Colin was moving the planchette just to freak out Aimee. I mean, the two of them were so weird last night.

"So, you got this on your own, Alex?" Dick's voice pulls me out of my daydreams.

I look at the fifteen pallets of dry goods waiting to be shelved. "Are you serious?"

"Well they don't call me the manager for nothin', I know how to delegate. Also, I have a life, loser. See ya!"

"They don't call you dick for nothin' either," I mutter under my breath.

Well, at this rate, I may be able to get to Aimee's right at the witching hour. That will give them a good scare.

*CLUNK!*

The noise breaks me from my thoughts. I really have to stop getting lost in my head.

"Dick?" I don't hear anything. "If we have another rat in here, I am leaving."

I walk towards the noise at the front of the store. As I reach the checkout, I see the open sign on the floor and realize the sound came from when it fell off the door. I pick it up and reattach the suction cup to the glass making sure that "closed" is the side that's facing out to the world. The only thing worse than being here all night stocking shelves would be if people kept knocking on the door every ten minutes thinking that we are open. I start back towards the aisle and the endless task ahead of me.

*KNOCK, KNOCK!*

"You can't be serious." I turn around, and sure enough, there is a man on the other side of the glass peering in at me. "And that's not creepy as fuck."

Wearing a cardboard Burger King crown and clothes that are ill-fitting, he looks like a crazed lunatic. *Is there any other kind of lunatic?* On his left arm is a tattoo of one of those mythological creatures that is made up of parts of other animals. He is just staring at me.

"Sir, we're closed."

He keeps staring at me.

"Fuck this, I have a job to do." I take one last look at Mr. King and tug the door to make sure it is locked. I fish around in my pocket for my headphones and head back to the pallets. I plug my headphones in to my phone, and just as I open my music app, my phone dings. Aimee is texting me.

*Is Colin with u?*

*No. At work still. Y?*

*He said he was on his way almost an hr ago*

*Maybe he got stuck at work. Did u call him?*

*I called. I'm worried.*

*I'm sure he's fine. I'll go to Bill's if he doesn't show soon*

*Can u go now? Pls*

*Ok. I'll check it out. Don't freak.*

I don't want to leave unless I have to, so I start calling Colin. He doesn't answer. I try the hardware store. There is no answer.

"Damn it! Fuck you, Colin. I don't have time for this shit." I throw my apron down on the open box of cereal. Bill's Hardware is a three-minute walk unless I take my time. If I don't clock out, at least I'll get paid for another fifteen minutes.

I start towards the front door but realize if King of Creep is still there, I'll have to interact with him. Best to go out the back door. I close the door carefully behind me so that he won't hear. If he's still there, he'll see me if I take the road so I walk down the alley to come out down the street and cut through the town square.

I stick my earbuds in and hit play on my phone. Capital Cities' *Safe and Sound* starts playing. Music is a solace these days. I put on a front for everyone. I tell the jokes, say I'm fine, but when I'm alone, music is the only thing that takes my mind off what happened.

My mom and dad were walking back to the car one night after dinner. Hard to believe, but they were still in love and acting like school kids and totally wrapped up in one another. They heard the car coming but didn't think it was going to jump the curb. The driver hit my mom straight on and kept driving. She didn't die right away and Dad didn't die at all, but he might as well have.

I am the only adult in the house now. Dad can't work due to his mental injuries. Even before it all, Mom was the glue that held us all together. Life can change on a dime, and I, like countless others, didn't realize that until it was too late.

OMI's *Cheerleader* is playing now, and I am almost to the other side of the square. I can see the hardware store and it looks like all the lights are off, but Colin's car is in the parking lot. The driver's door is open and the interior light on, but Colin is nowhere in sight. I take my earbuds out and approach the car. A quick look inside reveals that it is empty.

"Colin?" I give a shout and listen. Maybe he forgot something in the store.

I shut his car door and walk over to the entrance of the shop. I peer inside, but it is too dark to see anything but a shadow moving. I tug on the door, and it opens.

"Colin?" I call out to him before stepping into the darkness. "Yo, Col?"

I know the light switches are on the back wall so I use my phone to light the way. Music still plays from my headphones, and I pause Bunny Berigan's *I Can't Get Started* to listen to what's happening in the store. My phone dings. Aimee is checking on me.

*Have u found him?*

*Not yet. At bill's now.*

I hear movement in the back of the store. The light from my phone is not enough so I keep moving towards the switches. I flip them all on at once, and my eyes take a moment to adjust. I look towards where I had heard the movement but see nothing out of the ordinary. I am about to head to the back when I look down and see Colin cowering under the counter.

"Colin! Man, you scared me. Colin?" I walk over to him and grab his arm. He screeches and hits his head on the counter as he scrambles away from me. "Colin, it's Alex."

He carefully opens one eye and then the next. He jumps to his feet and rushes me with a hug.

"Okay, okay, get off me, man." I push him off me, but he keeps close. His need for human contact is apparent. "What's going on?"

"We summoned something." His voice is frantic. "There's something here. It's, it's…got red eyes, and it's after me."

I look around the store and see nothing but what belongs here. "Let's say I believe you. There's nothing here now. You're safe. And Aimee's worried about you. Let me help you lock up and then you can get over to her place." I guess I won't be scaring the shit out of them later; someone already did.

"That's just it. I can't lock the door! Then, it was in my car. I ran back here 'cause Bill keeps a shotgun under the counter, but that's gone."

"Colin, I was just at your car. Nothing was in there. Maybe Bill took the gun to clean it or just didn't trust you with it." He looks at me like my logic is good, but he just can't believe it. "Come on, where are your keys?"

"I, I don't know."

"Think! Where did you have them last?"

"The car. When I saw—" A shiver runs through him. "When I saw the eyes, I put the car in park and booked it back in here."

"The keys weren't in the car. Had you already locked up? You would have needed them to get back inside."

"Oh my God." His eyes widen, "I did lock up, but the door was unlocked. I…"

*Clink*

"What was that?" Colin jumps.

"Colin, calm down. I'll go look."

"No!" He grabs my sleeve. "Don't leave me here alone."

"Okay, then come with me."

With Colin holding on to me for dear life, we walk to the aisle where we heard the noise. Not wanting to freak him out further, I try to remain as nonchalant as possible. We round the endcap and there, in the middle of the floor, are a set of keys. My phone dings, and Colin pulls me towards the door.

"We gotta' go. C'mon." The panic in his voice is replaced with sheer terror.

"Colin, I don't know what's going on, but I think you're overreacting. Let me grab the keys, and we'll leave."

He lets go of my arm, and I walk over to collect the keys. Colin's behavior has me on edge and I expect something to happen as I crouch to pick them up, but the whole process is uneventful.

"Okay, let's go," he urges. He's already heading for the door so I head for the counter to shut off the lights. "Leave them. Let's just get to Aimee's."

It's not my job on the line, so I oblige.

We step outside, and Colin doesn't venture too far from me as I turn to lock the door. I rummage through his keyring to find the right one and sense him like an antsy child impatiently waiting for me. I finally find the right one, and after I pull it out of the lock, I look back through the window and search for something that would make Colin act this way. No red eyes stare back at me.

I hand Colin the keys. "Will you drop me back at the grocery store before you go to Aimee's?"

"You aren't coming with me?" He anxiously looks around the parking lot.

"I got work to finish." My phone interrupts our planning. I look at the screen. "It's Aimee. She's calling." I answer. "Hey, I've got him. He's weird though, like weirder than usual."

Aimee doesn't laugh.

"Alex, something weird is going on here." Aimee's texts didn't convey the fright that her voice does. "Will you both come over? Quick!"

The line goes dead.

"I guess I'm going with you," I tell Colin, and relief fleets across his face. "You're not driving though. Give me the keys."

He tosses me the keys and cautiously approaches the passenger side of the car. Peering in the back-door window at an empty seat, his fear is extinguished for the moment.

I climb into the driver's seat and start the engine. Still on edge, Colin gets in, and I throw the car in reverse. I look over at him as we pull out of the parking lot.

"Are you going to keep your eyes closed the whole way?"

"You don't get it, Alex. We brought something here. This is serious."

"What did ol' red eyes do to you that was so serious?"

"It... it was everywhere. In the store. In the car. It's playing with us. That's how it starts. Then we all die."

"Slow down. You've watched way too many scary movies. This *evil* didn't even do anything evil. You are overreacting."

"I'm not!" His eyes shoot open. "Watch out!"

I look back to the road and slam on the brakes. The car skids, and there's a crunch of metal. My head hurts, but I struggle to stay conscious as I wonder why the King of Creep was in the middle of the road.

## Colin

### Saturday, August 22 9:56pm

"Alex! Alex!" He crashed the car. My dad would kill me, but at the moment, I don't care. There had been a strange man in the road, but I didn't see red eyes before we veered off course.

I try shaking Alex, but he is out cold. I lost my phone back at the store. I unbuckle my seatbelt and search his pockets in the hope that his wasn't harmed in the crash. I find it, but my heart drops as I see "no service" across the screen. I shake Alex again. He is breathing but shows no signs of consciousness.

I hear heavy breathing that's not coming from him and look around the car. There is no one else here, and I realize the person breathing is me. I am hyperventilating. The close confines of the car remind me of all the times when my father locked me in the closet. I need space and air.

The door is stuck, but I push as hard as I can. It doesn't budge. I climb into the backseat and try the passenger's side door. It too is stuck, and I turn to my last option other than climbing over Alex. I have success, but the first few steps are rough and I stumble. I take a few deep breaths and regain some composure.

I look around and recognize my surroundings. I am about a ten-minute walk from Aimee's, five if I cut through the woods. I shudder at the thought of crossing through the dark trees on my own, but Alex needs help and I owe it to him to suck it up and go the short way. I try one more time to wake him and check his phone before shoving it in my pocket. Then with a childish fear, I head into the woods.

## Alex

### Saturday, August 22 9:59pm

***I'm not going to wake you again, Alex. If you don't get up, I'll throw you on the bus in your pajamas.***

"Mom?" I am groggy. My head hurts, but I hear my mom's voice as clear as day. I open my eyes. Even that simple action hurts. I see a steering wheel. There is broken glass and a deflated airbag. *A car crash*. I was in a car crash. I move quickly and am met with pain all over my body. There are no life-threatening injuries that I can see, but it is a struggle to remember what caused the accident.

Then I remember.

The man with the crown. King of Creep. He had been in the road, and I swerved when Colin yelled.

*Colin!* He isn't in the car. I reach into my pocket for my phone, but it isn't there. I manage to get my seatbelt off, and with blurred vision and searing pain, I search around the floor of the car and between the seats. But I can't find it.

The door creaks as I exit the wreck. I keep a hand on the car to steady myself as I take my first steps, hoping that nothing is broken. My limbs seem fine, but the world will not stop spinning. I close my eyes, but that makes the dizziness worse. Climbing up the embankment, I keep my eyes focused on the road sign so they won't wander and make my head hurt more.

I reach the road in one piece, but it could be hours before

another car travels this stretch. I don't see the King anywhere, and that's the only comfort I have right now.

"Colin!"

If he is still here, he doesn't respond. With how scared he had been, I can't imagine he wandered off on his own, but if he didn't, the other options running through my mind are not favorable. My best bet is to keep walking on the road. Maybe someone will come along, and if not, I am almost to Aimee's.

I put one foot in front of the other, my motto these days. It's amazing what a human being can survive. It's tragic what a human being cannot. I hear footsteps not my own shortly into the walk. I don't want to turn around for fear that I know who they belong to.

The quicker I walk, the closer they sound. I am at full speed in my post-car crash state, and I know I can't compete with a snail right now, much less whatever is on my tail.

I stop and turn to face my pursuer, expecting an old man with a crown, but no one is there. I search the landscape, but I can't see anyone. *Is this why Colin was going mad?* For the first time tonight, I start to believe we may have conjured up something then I turn back around and have my proof.

"Mom?" I ask.

"Hiya, sweetie."

"Are you real?" I reach out to her, but my hand meets empty space.

"That's such a wishy-washy term."

"Did I die in the crash?"

"No, but I wish you did." She grins unlike my mother. Hell, unlike any living creature.

"What?" I back away from her.

"You are in pain. There would be no pain if you were dead."

"It's manageable." Something, other than the fact I am talking to my dead mother, is not right. "Why are you here?"

"To help."

"To help me how?"

"I never said to help *you*."

Her grin turns to a malicious scowl. I muster up enough strength purely through adrenaline and plow through her. I don't know if I'll have enough energy to make it to Aimee's but her house is the only place for miles and, therefore, my only hope.

## Colin

## Saturday, August 22 10:20pm

I am lost. I am not an outdoorsy guy. I can't follow the stars. I can't even follow directions. I have walked through these woods with Aimee, but always during the day. At night, all the trees look the same, and I can only hope I am heading in the right direction.

*Snap!*

I stop moving and crouch, listening for whatever made the sound. All I can hear is my blood pumping and my ragged breathing. Surely whatever is after me can hear the same. Maybe my luck this evening will change and it's Alex coming after me. I wait a while longer, hoping not to see those red eyes. Seconds pass, but each feels like an hour. Deep inside is the urge to move and get help for my friend, but self-preservation is winning out tonight. I feel trapped, like a mouse on a glue strip. If I move, surely a part of myself will be left behind for vultures to scavenge.

Trapped is not a new feeling, but the terror that accompanies it tonight is unbearable. The weight of it all is exacerbated by the fact that, tomorrow, I am supposed to be free.

The plan was to be out of my father's house and away from his fist. I was going to be free from Aimee, a girl I could never truly love despite my father's wishes and her romantic ideals. I was going to be out of this town and away from the past of it that haunts me every day I stay. All these plans, though, depend on if I survive right now.

Alex, he's always been there for me in his own way. I owe him. I can't say that the support has been reciprocal. When his mother died, I pulled away for several reasons. My father didn't approve of Alex's newfound poverty. I could be here for him now if I could just get my sorry ass off the ground.

I push myself up and throw caution to the wind. Hurdling over fallen trees and dodging branches, I charge in the direction that I hope will lead to Aimee's house. My lungs are stressed from exertion instead of fear, and the burning in my chest feels good.

There is a clearing up ahead, and as soon as I reach it, I feel like the fates are on my side. Like a lighthouse on a rocky shore, Aimee's house stands as a beacon of hope and safety. Finally clear from obstacles of nature, my run towards the house is made easier. I know where the key is, but I try the back door first. It is unlocked. *Surprise.* I enter and call out,

"Aimee?"

I get no answer, but the lights go out and the only thing to light my way are those damn red eyes.

# Alex

## Saturday, August 22 10:20pm

"Fuck"—I pant—"me." My legs won't keep moving, and I fall to the pavement. My head hurts far worse than I ever thought imaginable. Maybe "not Mom" was right. At least dead people don't feel. That was obvious since whether that thing was some true variation of my mom or not, it had no feelings.

I am so disoriented and have no clue how far I've already run. With no road signs or landmarks I recognize in the dark, it is hard to tell where I am. I've been to Aimee's thousands of times, even on foot after I had to sell my car, but right now everything looks unfamiliar. I fall to my knees. I feel like lying down and sleeping right here in the middle of the road, but I've come too far to give up now.

"Alex," my mother's voice tempts from afar.

I push myself up on one knee. The most unsettling aspect of this all is that something demented looks and sounds like the person I love most. It taints my memories of her, which are all I have left. I can hear her getting closer and use all my strength to get on my unsteady feet.

"Alex, are you ready?"

"Not for you, bitch," I mutter.

Inches are milestones as I trudge along this stretch of blacktop. I don't know what I hope to accomplish since whatever follows me probably has the ability to show up anywhere at will, but I've been an underdog long enough now a part of me hopes I'll overcome.

Then, a terrifying thought bursts from the back of my mind. *I still have to stock the shelves after all this.*

I start laughing. Either my sense of humor is still intact,

or delirium is setting in far worse than I thought. Sarcasm gets me through all life's tragedies, so regardless, I'm glad my old friend is still by my side.

"What's so funny, Alex? Tell Mother." Her voice sounds farther away, and I feel hopeful that my perseverance is paying off in this chase.

With my spirit lifted, albeit unwarranted, I pick up the pace. The pain doesn't seem so bad if I keep moving. I try to fill my head with other thoughts and find myself drawn to the last time with my mom.

It wasn't tragic. I didn't say anything I regret. There were no harsh words. It was a typical Friday night, and when I said goodbye, I never imagined it would be for the last time. I called it my *Our Town* memory. I thought about how she looked and the way her arms felt wrapped around me as she hugged me. I did regret all the times before when I shied away from her embrace in public. All to save face, I missed out on so many extra chances to feel her love.

"Alex." Her voice breaks into my thoughts, and my short triumph is shattered as I look straight ahead and see her blocking my path to Aimee's.

"Move," I grit.

"Don't talk to your mother that way!"

"You're not her. Now move!"

"Not until you answer one question."

"Nah, I'm good. I know how this shit works. I answer and win a free trip to Hell or some shit." In my head I move with much more bravado, but I am sure reality looks much more pathetic.

"Answer the question, Alex, and you can save your friends."

I pause.

"So selfless, my son."

"Don't call me that! I can save them without your help."

"So sure of yourself. Just a short time ago, you were sure that Colin was crazy. What do you think now?"

"Is that the question? 'Cause I've always thought that Colin was crazy." I limp past her.

"Time is running out, and you know all about time running out, don't you?"

"Leave me alone!" I make my move to Aimee's. All the lights are on inside, but I see no movement. My turtle's pace suffices until all the lights go out inside, and pain tears through me as I race towards the house.

Not Mom calls after me, "How will justice be served?"

## Aimee

## Friday, August 21 8:02pm

"Alex is on his way over. He finally got out of work." I think Colin is more excited to be with him than he is to be with me. It's not the first time I've felt this way. Here we are, on the cusp of freedom, heading off to college, and I am probably the only virgin left in our town. Well, me and Colin if he hasn't done the deed with someone else.

In the beginning, it was nice being with Colin. I appreciated that he didn't pressure me like I'd heard other boys did. Now, we have been dating four years and even heavy make-out sessions are few and far between. It would have been nice to go off to college with some experience, but I don't see that happening tonight.

"I found this in my parents' closet. We should use it." I

hold up the dusty box with a Ouija board contained in its tattered confines.

"Seriously?" He disapproves as he does of most excitement. I would never tell him, but he was becoming more and more like his father every day.

"Are you afraid?" I try my best to tease him lightly. I don't want to spend the evening with a grumpy bore.

"Of course not, but you shouldn't mess with those things. Bad shit can happen."

"Oh my God, you're right. It already did. You swore."

"Ha ha." But Colin is not amused.

"Really, what would your father say?"

"Can we not talk about him?"

I see that just the mention of his dad can ruin the evening. "Yeah. But seriously, you don't really believe in all this ghost stuff, do you?"

"Well, why would it be fun if you didn't believe?"

"Hmm, you have me there." I throw my arms around his neck and place a kiss on his lips. He doesn't pull away, but he doesn't deepen it. "We just have to follow the instructions, and we will be safe."

He is still reluctant, but he's always been one to go with the majority. All I have to do is convince Alex, and Colin will be game.

"Hello, hello!" Alex let himself in the front door. "I come bearing expired food and drink. Who dares consume these perishing perishables?"

"Whatcha' got?" I grab the grocery bag from him and peek inside at my options. I get a root beer and some chips and leave the rest on the counter for the boys. Colin fishes around and pulls out a sports drink and some chips.

"You'll never guess what Aimee wants to do tonight." Colin is hoping Alex won't be on board.

"Watch porn?" Alex asks.

I hit Alex playfully on the arm, and Colin shifts uncomfortably at the suggestion.

"No," Colin chastises Alex and points the Ouija board box I left on the table. "She wants to use that."

"Can't we do both?" Alex likes to joke, but I think this time he is serious. Truthfully, I wouldn't mind doing both, but it's easier to settle for the one we can get Colin to agree to.

"Can't we just watch a bad scary movie and eat expired junk food?" Colin's still fighting to be a bore.

"Ya scared, Col?" Alex pops one of Colin's chips in his mouth, even though he could get his own bag.

"He claims not to be," I chime in on their banter. Colin stares us down, realizing he has lost.

"Fine, but if anything weird happens, we stop. I don't need to be bringing some spirit with me to Duke."

"Who would follow you when they could stay here with me and haunt my exotic life as a grocer?" Alex says. "If we channel any dark spirits, my life will feel just like home to them."

"Home sweet Hell." I do feel bad that Alex is stuck here. I can't wait to leave and not look back at any of this. "Come on, boys, let's talk to the dead."

I place some candles around the living room and then dim the lights. Alex sets the board up on the floor, and we circle around it. Colin is reading the instructions on the back of the box like he is studying a great philosophical work. He furrows his brow, and Alex and I give each other a look.

"So, Colin, how does this thing work?" Alex asks. "We need batteries or do the spirits come charged?"

Colin gives Alex the side-eye.

"I just want to be sure we're doing it right."

"Okay then." I am anxious to start. "How do we do it?"

Colin sets the box behind him and places his fingers on the planchette.

"Only two people should use the board." Colin, the expert, states.

"I'm in then!" Alex places his fingers next to Colin's before I can even move.

"Hey! I'm the one who wanted to do this in the first place!" I am annoyed that the boys always take the fun away from me.

"Relax, baby." Colin throws out the terms of endearment only when there are others around to hear. He is really laying it on thick tonight as he uses his free hand to hold mine. "You can still ask questions."

"Okay, what should we ask?" I sip my root beer and wait to hear what stupid ideas they have.

Surprisingly, Colin is the first to speak. "We are supposed to introduce ourselves, so I'll go first. Hello, spirits, my name is Colin."

"Howdy, Casper! You can call me Al."

I laugh. Colin does not.

"If anyone is listening, I'm Aimee. We'd like to chat with

you."

"Okay." Colin takes command. "I'll ask a question first. Will my move to college go smoothly?"

"Seriously, man? You got the world of the unknown at your fingertips and that's your question?" Alex looks peeved.

"It is a serious question, and I expect a serious answer."

Alex shakes his head, and I hold back a yawn in the most dramatic fashion. We all keep our eyes on the planchette. Nothing happens.

"Colin, you're so boring, you put the dead to sleep."

"Okay, Alex, what question do you have for the great spirits?" Colin asks.

I cringe at Colin's insensitivity. Alex plays off his mother's death like it's no big thing, but I can see the hurt on his face.

"How about this?" Alex takes a moment to contemplate. For a second, it looks like he doesn't want to say the words out loud. "Is my mom at peace?"

Colin and I share a look now. Our class clown doesn't show his soft side often.

The flames from the candles flicker slightly. The planchette starts moving. I didn't think Colin had it in him to be kind, but I see it move to the "yes" on the board.

"Very funny, Colin." Alex doesn't seem upset.

"It wasn't me." Colin looks petrified, which leads me to believe he is telling the truth. I don't think Alex would answer his own question, at least not that one.

"It's working then. Ask something else!" Alex is giddy like a little boy.

"I've got one." I regret asking before the words even leave my mouth. "Will I get laid before I leave for college?"

Colin's eyes shoot daggers at me, but I thought we could use a little levity and confession after Alex shared a tender moment with us.

"Wait, you two haven't…"

"Shut it, Alex! Why would you ask that, Aimee?"

"Well, you can't seem to answer that question." I hadn't been trying to start a fight, but I succeeded nonetheless.

"Hey, guys." There is a nervousness in Alex's voice that I am not used to hearing.

The planchette is moving. The boys leave their hands on it, and the candles start flickering more. My hand is still in Colin's, and I squeeze his tightly. The planchette creeps along to the *e* then to the *t*. It pulls away and then heads right back to the *t* and then moves to the *u*.

Colin takes his hand off the planchette and stands up abruptly.

"Enough! This isn't a game. I'm done!"

"Colin, I don't think you're supposed to walk away." The planchette has stopped moving now, and the candle flames remain still. "I think you're supposed to say goodbye or something," Alex calls to Colin as he walks towards the door.

"Goodbye." Colin doesn't stop or turn around, and when he gets to the front door, he yanks it open and slams it shut behind him.

"I'm sorry, Aimee." Alex's fingers are still resting on the planchette as he tries to figure out how to handle the awkward situation.

"It's not your fault. I made him mad. He'll come back anyway. His keys are on the counter."

"Well, maybe I should go. The mood he's in, if he sees me stay any longer, he'll probably think I'm helping you answer your question."

My head starts to hurt.

"Huh?" I ask, even though I heard what he said.

"About getting laid. Are you okay? You just got really pale."

"Yeah, I'm—" I can see clearly and I know what I want to say, but the words don't come and I can't help but stare. I am not staring at Alex but past him. I snap out of it. "I'm okay. Just tired."

"Sure?"

"Yes." I offer a smile.

"All right, well, call me if you need something. When do your parents get back?"

"Why? You wanna' sneak into my bedroom tonight and ravage me?" I don't know where that came from, but even more shocking is that a part of me really wants to know.

"Um, no. I think you are acting weird, and I don't want to leave you alone."

"Oh," I hear the disappointment in my voice, but I am not sure that Alex does. "They'll be back on Sunday. When Colin comes back in, I'm sure we'll make up. I'll be fine." Skeptically, Alex gathers his things.

"All right, well, call me if you're not. Night."

I sit down on the couch and hear the door close as he leaves. I know Colin will be back as soon as he sees Alex drive off so I brace myself for the argument. A pointless argument for sure, since we both know this relationship is just for show.

The door opens and closes gently.

"Aim?" The softness in Colin's voice is startling. "I'm sorry."

"You're sorry? I pick a fight, and *you're* sorry? You're pathetic." The harshness that comes from me is just as startling and made worse since I don't know why I am saying these things.

"I know I am. I know I've been leading you on and that makes me pathetic and an ass."

I am astonished to hear him speak the truth.

"You deserve someone who wants to be with you. Don't get me wrong—I care for you, but I don't love you." It's as if someone unlocked the floodgates and his true feelings are finally escaping.

"Are we breaking up?"

"Yes." I should be crushed, but I feel nothing.

"Okay. Wanna come over tomorrow?"

"Are you okay, Aimee?" The look of concern on his face is the most interest he's shown in me since freshman year.

"Great. I just thought since you have no one else, you'd like to spend your last night in familiar company."

"My last night?"

"In town. Before you leave for North Carolina."

"Oh, sure. We can hang out. No Ouija board though." He chuckles nervously.

"Yeah, that was pretty lame. You better go. Your dad will rip you a new one if you're late."

"You're right, but really, no hard feelings."

I smile, and even though I can't see my face, I picture how creepy I must look. "No hard feelings."

He grabs his keys from the counter and exits in the same fashion he entered.

After that, I remember nothing until morning when I wake up naked on the front lawn.

I feel better than I ever have, but I also feel like I am someone else entirely. All the rage simmering inside me has come to a boil, but I wear it on my sleeve like a glittery unicorn under a rainbow. I feel as though I've been asleep for thousands of years and I have finally been rescued from my slumber. Now, I am ready to live.

## Colin

### Saturday, August 22 10:42pm

Those red eyes follow me as I run back to the door. It is locked now. I push and pull and beat and bang, and the thing will not budge.

Even though I can't see who the eyes belong to, I feel them behind me. They are burned into my brain, and I don't need eyes to see them vividly.

"Oh God, oh God."

Futile, I know, but I just keep trying the door.

"Aimee?" I shout, hoping she's still alive for completely selfish reasons. My eyes are closed, and I feel warm breath on my neck. I know in this moment that my actions have finally caught up with me. I am going to die.

I turn to face my fate and slowly open my eyes just in

time to see light streaming in from the moon. A limping Alex bursts through the front door.

# Alex

## Saturday, August 22 10:44pm

"Aimee? Colin?" I don't even feel the pain now. It's still there like some foggy memory trapped in the far recesses of my mind, but adrenaline has hit me full force. I wonder if my dad had been given this gift if he would have been able to pull my mom from harm's way.

"Alex!" Colin's voice reaches me. It's so dark I can't see anything, but I know my way around the house and know that his voice came from the back door. I weave my way through the kitchen and can just make out Colin's shadow. He grabs me tightly.

"Where's Aimee?" I ask.

"I don't know. Something is definitely here though. We need to get out of here."

"Let's find Aimee, and then I'm right behind you."

I make a move to go upstairs, but Colin's hold is tight and the adrenaline is fading. "Colin, we have to find Aimee."

He doesn't move. I can't see his face, but I feel his inner conflict. Finally he speaks. "You're right."

Without letting go, he follows me upstairs.

"Aimee? Are you up here? It's Alex and Colin," I say.

A creak comes from her bedroom. The door is open, and moonlight flitters through the crack between the billowing curtains.

We enter the room and I hope to find her hiding in the closet or under the bed, but she is not here. Just as I am about to lead the way out of the room, the door slams closed, and we both turn around quickly to find Aimee standing between us and the doorway.

"Hello, boys." She is dressed very provocatively, and if we weren't in the current situation, things might be playing out more like a porno than a terrible slasher flick. But nothing kills the mood so much as near-death experiences, demonic otherworldly beings, and the sheer terror being expelled from the boy hanging on my arm.

"Hey, Aims. What's going on?" I ask.

"Cute. You know what's going on. You're a smart boy."

"Thanks for the compliment, but I really haven't a fuckin' clue."

"Are ya scared?"

"No. I'm pissed." And I am.

"I'm terrified, Aimee." Colin utters.

"You should be." Her voice gets low, and she takes a step towards us.

"Aimee, what happened here? What happened to you?" I ask. Colin hides behind me as she gets closer.

"Oh, Alex. What happened is that I've opened my eyes to the world. I see every nasty truth, and I think you should too. What do you think about that, Colin?"

"I don't really know what you're talking about," he says.

I get the feeling that he does.

"Sure you do. I think we should tell Alex all about it."

"No!" Colin *does* know, judging by that reaction. "You can't know anything about that. I never told you. I never told anyone!"

"No, you never told me much of anything. But you did tell me you hit a deer that night you showed up with a banged-up car covered in blood. That was a lie though, wasn't it?"

"Please stop." Colin is sinking to the floor slowly, and the truth starts to sink in for me.

"How did your dad react to that? Oh, that's right," Aimee gets closer, and I feel less inclined to protect Colin. "He beat your ass. Imagine if he knew what—no, *who* you hit. Are you getting the picture here, Alex?"

The picture is clear. I fill with pure hatred. I'd often thought about the type of person who could drive away after hitting someone, and I'd never pictured Colin. I pry his fingers off my shirt. Rage overtakes pain and reason.

"What do you think we should do with Colin?" Aimee's voice is playful.

"Please, Alex. I'm sorry," Colin says. "It was an accident. I swear. I was high and had poor judgement. I'm so sorry."

"You're so sorry?" I am surprised at how calm my voice sounds. "You didn't step on my toe or not hold the elevator. You killed my mom!"

Now, I dig my fingers into him. Strength pours out of me as I lift my former friend off the floor. Tears stream down his face.

"Do you want to kill him?" Aimee wants me to.

"Yes," I grit through my teeth.

"You should. He'd do everything exactly the same if it

happened again. Knowing him, it will happen again.”

“No, no, I wouldn’t,” Colin cries. “I, I, I wouldn’t.”

“Shut up!” I need to think, and my head is pounding. It would be so easy to push him out the window. I wonder if the force from the second floor would feel the same as his car plowing into my mom. I have visions of his head splattering below on the patio.

“Alex,” Aimee puts her hand on my arm as if to comfort me. “Your mother will never find peace until justice is served.”

“Justice? What is justice?” I say. “How can he ever truly pay for what he did?”

“With his life.”

“No, no, please,” Colin says. “I’ll turn myself in. I’ll go to jail. That’s justice. Please, Alex.”

“Stop pleading.” I drag him to the window with little effort.

But he says, “You’ll regret it all your life, man. Trust me, I know.”

“Well, I’ll live to regret it. You won’t.”

He struggles and puts his arms out to stop from going out the window. My absolute disgust for him takes over, and I bash his head into the windowsill. He goes limp.

Aimee starts clapping like Tiger Woods just sank a putt on the back nine. Apparently, murder is a spectator sport.

“Throw out the trash.” A Cheshire Cat grin takes over her face.

I look down at my mother’s murderer. *How will justice be served?*

I could take him to the police. He’d get prison time.

With his dad's money and reputation, he'd get out early or get off completely. Maybe this would change him.

Or I could kill him, and he can burn in Hell. After recent events, I am absolutely sure it exists. But then, do I go to Hell for what I've done?

"Alex, he killed your mom," Aimee says.

"I don't need a reminder."

"He lied to you for months."

"I'm aware." All at once I have Aimee's urging and my mother's voices in my head. My real mother wouldn't want me to take a life. The literal devils on my shoulder do. More importantly, I want to.

Aimee must see the look in my eyes because she gets giddy. "Want some help? I'm ready to lend a hand."

"No." I don't recognize who is talking, but as soon as I pick up Colin and throw him out the window, I realize the word came from my lips.

*SPLAT!*

"Oooh, feels good, don't it?"

I expected that it wouldn't, but it does. I expected remorse, but there is none. I expected guilt, but I feel free. I never expected justice, but I have it.

I laugh. Aimee laughs with me.

# Biddeford Weekly Journal
### Biddeford, September 25, 1891

## Saco River Not Only Cursed Landmark

The charred ruins of an old cabin
in Saco revealed the remains of an
Indian thought to have been trapped
in the structure years ago. Residents
have avoided the area due to stories
over recent years of hunters disappearing
from the woods surrounding the cabin.
The body was discovered due to local
philanthropist, Alden Hilt, clearing the
land to build a summer house on the
property. Mr. Hilt did not comment
on whether he thinks the land is cursed,
but locals are convinced the land
should be avoided. Many lives are lost
to the curse of the Saco, and in this
case, only time will tell if myth
can be taken as truth.

There is something about a house with a turret that just sends chills through my spine. It is a characteristic of many old haunted houses, including the one before my eyes. Night has fallen on the town and over this historic building. The brown edifice is creepy enough during the day, and now with the darkness encompassing the building, it seems like all hope is lost.

From the brightly lit street, I approach the dark hole. Cars zoom by behind me, and from my peripheral vision, I see headlights every now and then. But it all fades away with each step I take.

The icy snow crunches under my feet. Each step is harder as the snow gets deeper. Although my shins are protected by boots, the little bit of snow that seeps in over the top is enough to make the trek even more uncomfortable. With every move, the snow crawls deeper and deeper down my boots.

Though just off the street, the house is still surrounded by trees. Four frosted shrubs are in front, and the pine trees all around are covered in a dusting of snow.

It seems as if the second my feet leave the pavement, I enter The Black Forest and a world unknown to man. No one lives here. The snow is unbroken except for my footprints. There is no path. Life does not exist here. Standing back from the building with the wind and cold burning my face, I look up in the window on the pointed turret. Curtains that were once white block the view to the inside; they are the only colorful thing emanating from inside the house, but they are yellowed from age and not the pure white they once were.

I move closer to the front of the house. The front door is the same brown as the rest of the house with black hinges on the screen door. The porch light is dusty and broken, and the glass crunches under my feet. The house number reads 201, but the 2 hangs upside down and, with each gust of wind, blows back and forth squeaking as if waving "hello" or perhaps "goodbye."

I open the screen door, and a gust of wind sends it flying open, hitting the side of the house and bouncing back. I open the next door, the metal knob like ice on my hands. I walk in the house, and as the door creaks behind me, I enter a world of perfect silence. The wind stops blowing, and now I am in complete darkness as the door slams shut behind me.

-

*"I bet there isn't a kid in this town that would even step foot on the yard, much less step foot in the house."*

*"Bullshit, Ricky. I bet we could find someone to prove his worth."*

*"With all the stories about the Hilt House, I wouldn't do it if you paid me a million bucks!"*

*"I'd do it if you paid me ten bucks. They are just stories. No one really died there. My dad has been a cop in this town for twenty years, and he said the only thing he has ever been called out there for is vandalism."*

*"That's 'cause your dad is trying to protect you, Tim. The stories are true. Every family that has lived there since it was built in the 1800s has died. That's why no one lives there anymore. But hey, if you'll do it for ten bucks, you could report back and let us know the truth."*

*"You want me to go there by myself?"*

*"Yeah, you are the one who said they are just stories."*

*"Maybe in the spring. It's too cold now."*

-

As my eyes try to adjust to the blackness, I catch shadows moving across the room. To my left is a staircase that I assume leads up to the top of the turret. To my right is a table that is dusty and falling apart, only three legs left to keep it standing. Underneath the table is part of a chair, and in the kitchen is the other half, scattered across the floor. A fridge lay knocked over with the door wide open and its moldy contents spewing out like entrails on the floor.

I tiptoe to my left and up to the turret that called me here on this chilly winter night. I step on the first stair and lean on the railing, which falls to the ground with an enormous clatter, breaking the silence as the house urges me to shush. I catch myself and proceed to the next step and the next, and with each step, the boards feel like they are ready to cave and send me to the fiery depths of hell. The warmth would surely be welcome at this point.

My eyes are finally adjusting as I reach the door at the top. I turn the old knob, but it is locked. I look at it closer and find a skeleton key already in the door. I turn the key and hear the clicking of the tumblers.

-

*I hear my brother Ricky and Tim talking. I wish Ricky would include me in things like he used to. Even though I am four years younger, I am mature for my age. I don't know when it became uncool for Ricky to hang out with his younger sister, but I miss him.*

*We used to play baseball in the back yard and make mud pies in the sandbox. He used to let me play videogames with him and read me stories before I could make out the words myself.*

*Now, I am in the way. I am childish. I am "just his younger sister."*

*Maybe, if I did what he and Tim were too afraid to do, he would think I was neat again. I could be back in his graces if only I could prove my worth.*

-

I walk in the room, which seems dustier than the rest of the house as if it had been hidden from the world longer than the other parts. I move to the window, pull the yellow curtains aside, and look out on the street. It seems empty now, and a streetlight that lit my way in must have gone out, leaving the one stretch of road as dark as the house. I let the curtain go, and dust flies off, filling my lungs. The curtain swings back and forth like the 2 from outside, and the smell of mold fills my nostrils and burns my lungs as I notice that the wall behind the curtains is cracked and damp. The back side of the curtain is covered in dark, gooey gunk that must have rubbed off the wall.

The ceiling is crumbling just like the rest of the building. The window on the other side has a crack running through it, which leads to a spiderweb of cracked glass in the middle as if someone had thrown something or punched the window. There is no blood so it seems more likely that something was thrown. I can just make out the tracks I left below in the snow, but there is more than one set of footprints now. It is time to go.

-

*"Wanna' play* Left 4 Dead*?"*

*"Yeah. I gotta' make sure my sister isn't burning down the house though. See if you can find the third controller, and I'll see if she wants to play with us. You cool with that?"*

*"Yeah, man. You always scare the witch and get us all killed!
She is the only one who tiptoes past so that we can actually survive."*

*"You know what? Just for that, there is going to be some friendly
fire. I just might mistake you for a zombie."*

*"Not cool, dude!"*

*"Tim! She's gone."*

*"Calm down, Ricky. What do you mean she's gone?"*

*"She left a note. She went to the Hilt House. She said she is
going to prove it's not haunted. My parents are going to kill me. Shit!"*

*"We'll just go get her. It's only a ten-minute walk, and she
can't have left too long ago. Relax, she's fine."*

-

I turn to leave but catch my boot on a board sticking up. I
fall hard and instantly feel warmth above my eye, and pain fills
my body. As I try to push myself up, I fall back to the floor with
a thud, and the last thing I hear is the door creaking shut and the
clicking of the tumblers falling back into place. Then the
darkness becomes darker, and a blanket of blackness covers me.
The house envelops me.

-

Ricky and Tim stare up at the turret that has spooked all
of Saco for the last hundred years or so.

"All right," Ricky says. "We go in, grab Rachel, and get
the hell out of here before we get killed."

"Sounds like a good plan to me."

They follow Rachel's tracks and head into the dark and
deserted house. They hope that once they make it inside the cold
will leave their bones, but even being out of the wind, the inside

of the house is colder.

"Stories or not, this place is creepy as…"

"Fuck!"

Tim and Ricky both jump as they hear a loud bang from upstairs. They look at each other and then to the staircase.

"Your sister is either the coolest kid on the planet or the stupidest," Tim says.

"I vote the last one. Let's go up the ramshackle stairs. What's the worst that could happen?"

"Just don't scare the witch."

Ricky hits Tim on the arm, and they inch closer to the staircase.

"You go first," Tim says, and Ricky glares at him. "You're smaller and these steps look bad. And, she's your sister."

"Rach! Rachel?" Ricky starts up the steps, and they creak and moan with every move. The door at the top of the stairs is open. "I think she's up here."

"Okay. Get her, and let's go home."

Ricky coughs as he enters the room. He sees a foggy circle on the window facing the street. Someone breathed on the window not long before Ricky entered the room. The other window is cracked.

"Rachel, come on. Let's go home."

Silence washes over Ricky. He looks carefully around the room for a hiding spot but sees no place where Rachel could be. He does see a spot of blood on the floor. He crouches down and touches his fingers to the red pool. It is fresh and warm and most likely his sister's.

"Rachel this isn't funny. We gotta' go!" Panic is in his voice. She isn't up here.

He runs back down the stairs, almost falling at least half a dozen times. Hoping Tim will know what to do, Ricky searches frantically for him. Tim is no longer at the bottom of the stairs.

"Tim? Rachel?" Silence.

-

Ricky has to go home. He told his parents that if they got him a cellphone, he would use it responsibly and then they would be able to check up on him whenever they wanted to. They didn't think he needed one.

Now, he runs from the Hilt House, trying to make the ten-minute trip in half the time. His lungs are burning. His legs are on fire. His mind is racing.

His house is near. He sees the lamp on and the flicker of the television through the living room window. He and Tim must have left it on when they hurried out of the house. But his parents' car is in the driveway. They must have left dinner early.

Finally, as he reaches the walkway to his front door, he slows his pace. Gasping for air, he stumbles into his house. His parents are on the couch watching *Gunsmoke*.

"Hey, Rick. Where have you been? It's too cold and dark out for you to be playing outside." His dad doesn't look away from the television once.

"Guys, we need help. Rachel ran away to the Hilt House and Tim and I went to save her, and now both of them are missing." Ricky doesn't take a single breath as he urges his parents to get off the couch and help.

"Slow down, Ricky. What are you talking about?" His mother recites the words with no emotion.

"Mom? What's going on? We need to save Rachel and Tim." Ricky still cannot pull their gaze away from the television. A shootout between Matt Dillon and the bad guys has their full attention. "Dad, please. We should call Tim's dad. He'll know what to do."

"Rick, can't this wait? We are trying to watch this show."

"Dad, this isn't a joke. Rachel is missing!"

"Who is Rachel, honey?"

"Mom, what's going on? Why won't you guys help me? My sister is in trouble!"

"Look, Rick, stop with this. You don't have a sister. We are trying to watch this show. Why don't you go up to your room and play some of those videogames you like?"

Ricky pinches himself to see if he is dreaming. It smarts, and he sees the blood on his fingers. Rachel's blood. Something is wrong with his parents.

He is the only one who can save Rachel and Tim and he has no clue how to.

-

Ricky stands outside looking up at the turret that sent chills up my spine. My brother is here to save me. He is here to save Tim. But he can't. I don't want him to. If he comes back inside, he will never leave again. I know this now. Once the house becomes a part of your soul, your soul becomes a part of the house. I will him not to enter the house, and at the same time, I want nothing more than that he join me. I want him to play baseball with me and make mud pies. I want him to read to me and let me play videogames with him.

None of that will happen if he sets foot inside these walls. We will be together but farther apart than ever. I know Tim is here too. But I can't see him. The house separates loved ones. There are a lot of loved ones here.

I want to lock the door. I want to board the windows. I want to be loved by my big brother. If he comes back in the house, I know he loves me.

Ricky walks up the front steps towards the waving 2, and I know what I should have known all along.

My big brother loves me.

# Two Sides

## Danny

Danny left the house at the usual time on Monday morning, but there was no way he would make it to work on time. After he fed his cats and made sure they would be all set for a day of naps, baths, and feasts, he headed out the door. Traffic on the freeway was surprisingly light, and he made it to the off-ramp in record time. He pulled the visor down to shield his eyes from the rising sun and rolled down his window to enjoy the cool early morning air. All was right in the world, and he would be to work twenty minutes early at this rate. There would be just enough time to stop and pick up some doughnuts and coffee for his co-workers and settle into his desk before his boss came in for the morning report.

His mind drifted as the radio news report played softly in the background. The sun changed angles again, and just as he reached to adjust the visor, he saw a man in the middle of the road. He quickly slammed on his brakes, and when he realized that this action alone would not be enough, he swerved to the right to avoid cars in the other lane.

*CRUNCH!*

The airbag deployed and sent Danny back in his seat. Still conscious but a little confused, he assessed the situation. He didn't seem to have any broken bones, and other than a little blood coming from his nose, there were no other cuts or scrapes.

Suddenly he remembered the reason he crashed. He tore off his seat belt and ran out of the car. He saw what it was he crashed into; a bright red BMW was on the side of the road and now had the rear end completely smashed. He looked around and saw the man he swerved to miss running towards him.

"Are you okay!?" The man had a look of concern on his face that Danny thought might be for him but most likely it was for the car.

"Yeah," Danny responded, "I will be fine, not much damage to my car either. What were you doing in the middle of the road?"

"Well, I was driving along, and there was a turtle crossing. I pulled over to help him get across. Didn't you see my flashers on the car?"

"How could I see those when the sun is so bright? You are lucky I saw you in enough time." *There was no way this guy was blaming this accident on him,* Danny thought.

"Sorry, I didn't realize the sun was that bad. I was coming from the other way, and I turned around when I saw the turtle. I don't have a cell phone. Could you call the police?" Finally realizing how bad the damage was, the man walked over to his BMW and swore. He kicked the tire, which made the rear end sink a little more. "Really though, how could you miss the car? It's bright red! I am pale white, and you saw me!"

"Well, if you weren't in the road chasing the Ninja Turtles, I wouldn't have had to swerve to miss you!" Danny was getting mad now. Not only was he not going to make it to work in time, but he now had to deal with this turtle-loving asshole.

"Well you still would have had to swerve to miss the turtle, but I guess an ass like you would have just hit him!"

"I would have swerved, but at least your fancy BMW wouldn't have been in the way! I am calling the police now, and you better have good insurance 'cause not everyone can just afford to run out and get a new car like you!" Danny was enraged, and this rich snob was not helping him in the least.

He called the police to report the accident and decided to keep quiet until they got there before his anger got the better of him.

# Tucker

There was no way Tucker was going to make it to his job interview on time. Ever since his house burned down last week, everything seemed to be in a downward spiral. Actually, the downward spiral had been happening for a while. His life was like a country song; he had no home, his truck broke down, his wife left him for a woman a month ago, and he was laid off from the factory job that he had for twenty-five years. The only good thing he had going for him was that he still had his dog. Luckily, his brother was able to take the two in, and with the help of some rewards points from one of his maxed-out credit cards, he was able to get a rental car for the next few days. Even sweeter than that, the only car they had available was a brand-new BMW.

He wasn't too excited about the prospect of flipping burgers at the local diner, but when he saw the words *willing to train* next to the help wanted ad, he decided this was better than nothing. He needed some way to pay the bills. His alarm clock apparently did not feel the same way since it never rang. When he realized how late it was, he rolled out of bed, fed his dog Kamir, and made himself as presentable as possible.

Once he hit the road in his shiny borrowed wheels, he felt a little better. As long as he didn't hit any traffic, this was still doable. He was cruising along with the radio blasting when he saw something in the road. He slowed as he got closer and realized it was a turtle. The animal lover in him couldn't just leave the turtle there, so he turned the car around and parked it on the side of the road. He took a second to find the emergency lights and clicked them on then got out of the car and ran back to the turtle.

Just as he bent over to pick him up, he heard the squeal of rubber behind him. He picked up the turtle as he turned to see a car speeding at him. At what seemed like the last second, the car veered off to the right, and there was a loud crunch.

Tucker quickly ran the turtle to the side of the road and then ran back towards the accident. A man got out of the car and approached him.

"Are you okay!?" Tucker was immediately worried about the man when he saw blood coming from his nose.

"Yeah," the man responded weakly. "I will be fine, not much damage to my car either. What were you doing in the middle of the road?"

"Well, I was driving along and there was a turtle crossing. I pulled over to help him get across. Didn't you see my flashers on the car?" All his life, people had told Tucker he was too nice and nice guys finish last. Here he was, just trying to save a turtle from getting crushed, and now he caused this man to crash. *Now I am dragging others into my downward spiral,* he thought.

"How could I see those when the sun is so bright? You are lucky I saw you in enough time." The man seemed angrier now. Maybe he was not an animal lover.

"Sorry, I didn't realize the sun was that bad. I was coming from the other way, and I turned around when I saw the

turtle. I don't have a cell phone. Could you call the police?"
Tucker walked over to his car to give the man some space and
realized just how bad the damage was. This was just his luck,
there was probably no way insurance would cover this, and he
knew the rental car company would jack up the price of repairs.
He kicked the tire to trying to release some steam, but that only
made the rear end sag a little more. Anger rose as his cheeks got
hotter. "Really though, how could you miss the car? It's bright
red! I am pale white, and you saw me!"

"Well, if you weren't in the road chasing the Ninja
Turtles, I wouldn't have had to swerve to miss you!"

*Well, this man is obviously not an animal lover,* thought
Tucker. This angered him even more. This arrogant bastard
couldn't see that he was trying to do something nice.

"Well, you still would have had to swerve to miss the
turtle, but I guess an ass like you would have just hit him!"

"I would have swerved, but at least your fancy BMW
wouldn't have been in the way! I am calling the police now, and
you better have good insurance 'cause not everyone can just
afford to run out and get a new car like you!"

Astonished at how fast this had escalated, Tucker backed
off, the last thing he needed was to get decked by this guy, or
even worse, sued. It didn't look like he would make it to that job
interview after all.

# Good Fortune

Luke longed to get away from the city. He had been in Atlanta for five years now and not one day had he felt at home. He even chose Atlanta because of its reputation as a "city in the forest," but a city was still a city.

He loved his job as a software engineer for one of the most dynamic companies in the south, but after a while the big city life finally got to him. He didn't have a lot of friends due to his long work hours. And forget about having time for a girlfriend; although, he didn't mind the thought of taking out his new co-worker, Rebecca.

But he would never have the courage to attempt that. There was no way a girl that beautiful would go for a boy as plain as he was. No, the best he could do to escape the hustle and bustle was to enjoy his weekend showings of horror classics at the little theater down the street from his loft. But that was all about to change this week.

Finally, he was cashing in his vacation time and renting a cabin in a remote part of the Chattahoochee National Forest. It took him forever to find the perfect place and at least two weeks of paychecks to secure it. What is the point of making money though if you can't enjoy it?

"Don't get lost in the woods, Luke!" The ever-chipper and drop-dead gorgeous Rebecca shouted to Luke on his way out of the building.

"I calibrated my GPS last night, Bex. I think I will be able to manage just fine."

"You better be. We should grab a drink and you can tell me all about it when you get back." Her eyes lit up as a smile washed over her face.

"Yeah, sure, that sounds great," he said. When her smile continued and she held eye contact a little too long, it finally hit him. "Oh, you mean like a date?"

Her giggle made fire rush to his cheeks.

"Yeah, like a date." Rebecca pushed a strand of hair from her face, but the smile never left.

"I'd really like that. Have a good week, Bex!" Luke couldn't seem to get the smile off his face either as he left the building.

The sun was just setting as Luke sped around the curves of GA-60. He hoped to make it to the cabin before it was too dark to see anything, but in his giddiness over his date next week, he forgot his rain gear and his GPS and had to turn back twice.

The farther into the forest he got, the radio kept cutting out. He hit scan to try and find some station that would come through clearly and instead got a garbled mismatch of classic rock, news, and static.

In between Blue Öyster Cult's *Don't Fear the Reaper,* he could barely make out the radio announcer's voice. "Has escap…States Penitentiary…in Atlanta…last seen entering Chattahoochee National Forest near Blue…"

Luke gave up and shut the radio off, realizing he was too deep into the trees to get a radio signal. He drove in silence and tried to pay attention to the bumpy dirt road he had turned on about ten miles ago. He could hear each rock his tires kicked up and left in a new position on the road.

Then, from the corner of his eye, he saw movement in the trees. He battled with the urge to pull over and check it out or speed up and get away from whatever it may be. The coward in him chose the latter and immediately pressed down on the accelerator.

He glanced at his Garmin Montana 600 GPS which said it was only another mile to his destination. He trusted his calibration and loved Garmin GPS devices, but he had never used this one in the wilderness and was hoping its ability to work in remote locations was as reliable as his calibrations.

Another shadow flashed by on the left. Luke stopped the car abruptly and squinted out the window, trying to make out what kind of creature was following him. It was already too dark for him to see anything clearly so he kept eyes to the left and inched forward with the car. Everything was quiet.

"You have arrived at your destination!" The GPS broke the silence and made Luke jump.

He slammed on the brakes and took a moment to collect himself. After he calmed his breathing, he looked ahead at his home for the next week. The GPS did not fail him after all.

The log cabin was everything he was looking for to escape the city. He couldn't tell very well in the dark, but it looked like it had been built recently and made to look like an old log cabin. For as much as he was paying, he hoped that the inside looked as nice. Leaving the headlights on, Luke grabbed his backpack out of the passenger seat and walked briskly towards the front door. Still on edge, he kept scanning in every direction. When he reached the front door, he took a moment to listen.

*Silence.* He opened the door and peered into the darkness. *No electricity*, he remembered. He reached for the flashlight attached to his bag, and as soon as he turned it on, he knew he had found a winner.

There was a small kitchen to the left, a cozy living room with a fantastic fireplace, and a small bedroom in the back with a twin bed.

"This is just what I need," he said to himself. With the flashlight in his mouth, he set his bag down and started over to the fireplace.

First things first, he would start a fire.

As soon as he got the fire going, he went back to the car to collect his food supplies and shut off the headlights. He was collecting the food from the trunk when all off a sudden,

*SNAP!*

He spun quickly and shined the flashlight in every direction.

"It's just your nerves," he assured himself and found himself comforted by his own voice. Still, he rushed to gather everything he needed, and after slamming the trunk and turning off the headlights, he locked his car and started for the cabin. As soon as he looked back at the front door though, he saw his stalker.

For a moment, his blood ran cold, and he stopped in his tracks until he started laughing hysterically. The raccoon who was captured in the beam from his flashlight looked at him for a moment and then ran away from the cabin.

"Being stalked by a raccoon! I should tell Bex about that on our date. Everyone seeks a mate who practically pisses his pants over an animal." Luke continued to laugh at himself as he walked back into the cabin and shut the door behind him.

The fire was going strong and lit up the whole cabin except for the bedroom. Luke realized now that there was a hook hanging above the fireplace and a tea kettle on the mantel.

"Now *that* is exactly what I need. A hot cup of tea. Very

manly and rugged." He poured some of his water into the kettle and pulled out a bag of tea leaves. After he got the tea going, he went about unpacking a few things. He found a cup in his bag and grabbed a towel so he wouldn't be burned by the kettle. He poured himself a hot cup of tea and sat on the couch waiting for the near boiling tea to cool.

Suddenly, he heard a whisper, "I'm not a raccoon."

Luke knew it was crazy, but he thought that's what he heard. He looked at his steaming tea and put his ear closer to the cup. *Maybe it's like Rice Krispies*, he thought as he remembered the "snap, crackle, and pop" conversation from his bowl that morning. He waited with the steam heating his right ear, and then he heard something,

"I'm behind you," it whispered. At least that's what Luke thought until he realized he heard it in his left ear.

# Revolutionary

*My ghost story starts on a brisk autumn eve, as any respectable ghost story should.*

No one ever means to fall in love; it just happens. Cliché, I know. In all my years roaming the earth, I was always under the assumption that it would never happen to me. But in all those years, I have learned never to assume.

I was born in New Town, Pennsylvania in 1757. I was born a free black man, which didn't mean much in the mid-eighteenth century. If anything, I had to be more careful. Sometimes, I thought that white men only gave privileges so that they could take them away one day. I guess that's true of anyone in power.

I was luckier than most though. My mother died in childbirth, and I was taken in by a peaceful Quaker family. This would not have been the case for most black men, but my mother was white and as long as I kept my mouth shut and worked hard, folks would look past my less-than-white skin. By look past, I mean it was as if I didn't exist at all.

I came of age during a time when revolution was stirring and a new nation was blooming. I longed to be a part of the action, but my adoptive family frowned on violence. They weren't loyalists, but many of the Quaker families in the area were. They didn't believe in British rule; they just didn't want to rock the boat.

Shortly after my eighteenth birthday, news reached us

that the war had begun. British troops had attacked colonists in Massachusetts. More importantly, the colonists fought back that day. Tensions were high, and despite my Quaker upbringing and my family's objections, I wanted to be a part of the revolution. I was one of those foolish enough to believe that freedom from the British would mean freedom for all.

That summer, I joined the associators when they regrouped. It felt good to be involved in the cause, however, I was merely enlisted as the help. All anyone seemed to do was talk while I was busy serving these talking men. I couldn't have been farther away from the action. This didn't stop my family from wanting nothing to do with me.

A year went by, and then excitement came to New Town. General Washington made his headquarters in town after a battle at Trenton. Riding on the coattails of victory and finally seeing my opportunity to join the war on the frontlines, I officially enlisted and traveled with Washington's men to Morristown for the winter.

My three years in the continental army were both exhilarating and disappointing. I had many close calls and almost lost my life to smallpox. I returned home to New Town a changed and defeated man. The excitement I once craved left a bitter taste in my soul. I had seen death and brought death to many, and there was nothing exciting about either.

I got a job on a farm outside town and decided that my Quaker upbringing hadn't been all that bad. It wasn't peace with the world that I needed, but rather peace with myself. As it turns out, personal wars can be endless and all-consuming too.

*

It was a brisk autumn eve in 1781, when I found myself on Main Street in New Town. I had almost finished off a whole bottle of booze, but I was only a little drunk. I had been building up quite a tolerance since I returned from the battlefield. I heard hoofbeats raging down the street. At that hour, it was odd for a gang of men to be roaring through town. My first thought was that there was news that the war had finally ended.

The moon was not very bright, but I could make out six riders. I knew immediately these were the outlaws who had been stealing horses from farms around the area. I was right back in the heat of the action, and every nerve in my body was on fire as my bones screamed in agony to remove myself from the situation. The danger I tried to escape had caught right back up with me.

There I was, one semi-drunk and broken man, but I knew I had to stand up to this posse of outlaws. I waited until they were within throwing range and chucked the bottle in my hand at the first rider. I don't know who had been more stunned—he or I—that it hit him square in the temple.

Unfortunately, it did not break until it hit the pavement. Before I could make my stand, a shot rang out in the otherwise still night. The smell of gunpowder filled my nostrils, and with a few kicks and yells, the group continued on down the street as if nothing had stopped them in the first place.

Dumfounded by the interaction, I took a step, still unsure if I would find my way home or find some other place suitable to sleep for the night. I only made it that one step before I collapsed. A warm feeling rushed down my body, and I placed a hand on my chest. When I pulled it away, my hand was warm and sticky. I knew that this was the end.

The blood pooled in my lungs as I started to gasp for breath. In that moment I should have been panicked like a fish out of water, but some form of peace washed over me instead, and I lay on the pavement waiting to be set free. Once again the fool, I was wrong to believe that freedom from life would actually set me free.

*

I knew I was dead. It was the first thing I was ever sure of in life, or rather, death. That's what made it all the more confusing when a short time after the week I was shot, it felt like I was alive.

The entire week, I had been roaming the street where I died. I could only venture so far in any direction before I found myself right back in the same spot I had died. No one could see me, and I couldn't touch anything. I felt so cold inside, but other than that, I felt nothing.

Then, on the day before what the Catholics call All Saints' Day, I bumped into a man on the street. His name was John and he worked at The Court Inn. He had always been kind to me, even though the color of my skin meant he didn't have to be. He took two steps back from me and crossed himself before running back in the same direction from which he came.

It seemed that news of my death had spread. I couldn't have imagined it was an important story, but nothing spreads news better or more inaccurately than gossip.

While he was shocked to see me alive, I was shocked he saw me. I still felt the same, but maybe that certainty about death had been wrong. At the very least, it seemed as though I could again interact with the real world.

I kicked a wagon on the side of the street. It didn't hurt, but I saw it shake. I heard the thump. I saw the owner running at me and shouting. I wasn't about to stick around for an argument.

I ran as fast as I could and didn't look back until I realized that I had made it farther than any of my other attempts to leave Main Street.

I slowed down and took in my surroundings. Not only had I made it farther, but I had traveled all the way out of town and back to the farm that employed me when I returned home from the battlefield. Why I would return there, I had not a clue. Things had ended poorly between me and Mr. Thomas after he caught me drinking in the barn when I was supposed to be working. The situation got even worse when that same barn caught fire and I was the man to blame.

I saw Mr. Thomas outside talking to my replacement. I couldn't let him see me. Even if the news of my death hadn't reached him yet, his last words to me were, "Don't let me see you back here!"

That was quite lenient. Even though I wasn't anyone's property, black men had been hanged for less.

I had to make it to the tree line before he saw me. I would wait there until dark or even better, keep going and get out of New Town. My plan would have worked if Mr. Thomas' daughter hadn't seen me first. Hanna was playing near the woods with the dog. I remained still, hoping the dog engaged her enough not to pay attention to the man lurking in the woods. But that dog always had a nose for me.

*Bark! Bark! Bark!*

I know he was just being friendly, and it was my fault for feeding him scraps and gaining his admiration. I moved farther into the woods, but the dog was in pursuit and Hanna followed closely behind, despite her father's warnings about venturing into the woods. Ghost or not, Hanna knew I wasn't supposed to be there and as soon as she saw me, she yelled, "Papa!"

Before Papa could make it to the scene, I turned and ran

as fast as my legs would allow. The trees turned to shadows around me as the sun sank too low to light my way. I had no clue where I was.

I lost all track of time, but I knew I had to keep going. My lungs didn't burn like they would have if I were alive. My muscles didn't ache. The moon broke through and lit my way out of New Town. Hell, I could make it out of Pennsylvania. Then, in the blink of an eye, I was running on an empty street.

*Main Street.*

After that night, I hid every year on what would come to be known as All Hallow's Eve. All my life, I had wanted to be seen, and in my death, all that changed. I wanted nothing more than not to be seen.

*

Hiding is easy when you are dead, and being dead has its perks. I decided to use my afterlife to educate myself. While I was isolated to a half mile radius, give or take, I managed to keep up with all the events in town. Once I learned how to read, I felt like all the world was in my hands. There is a reason the white man feared what would happen if black men could read.

When the first library building was constructed, I spent all my days and nights there. It took me some time to figure out how to manipulate solid objects, and I always had to be careful when I was around living people. I didn't want to discourage reading by starting the rumor that the library was haunted.

The knowledge I gained through reading wasn't the only excitement that came into my life over time. The abolitionist movement was in the works. Being dead put a bit of a damper on what the fight for freedom would mean for me, but I felt I owed it to my brothers and sisters to do all I could to help them. I had the same giddy feeling as when I wanted to take up arms and join the revolution. That meant I also had a feeling of dread since that battle for the nation did not mean freedom for all.

Newtown, the two words had come together slowly over time, was mostly helpful to the cause. We helped many seeking a better life with the North on the Underground Railroad. I did my part by spooking horses of Southerners looking for runaways. Occasionally, I would come "out of hiding" to those who needed to be pointed in the right direction. My favorite pastime, however, was to yell in the ears of assholes from the South or even touch them. They might seem all high and mighty when they are chasing down a man with no rights, but they scream like babies when dealing with a ghost. A few guys even pissed their pants. I just wish I could have done more.

I was able to hear the words of Frederick Douglass and Lucretia Mott. The latter impressed me more. I think I was drawn to her because of my Quaker upbringing. It had been many years since my family had died, and even though they kicked me out of their lives, listening to Lucretia made me miss home. Or it made me realize I ever had a home to miss.

The war came. Men died. Freedom did not ring. Sure, emancipation was the law of the land, but when had law ever applied to rich white men? Slavery was only a part of the oppression. Chains and whips are not the only way to hold someone down and keep a man in line.

*

As hard as it is to believe, my world expanded. I was still confined to a small section of State Street, no longer Main Street, and the surrounding areas, but newspapers gave more national and global news. Then radio came, then television, and both seemed to take on an important place in the homes of my fellow Pennsylvanians.

I saw so much come and go and yet so much remain the same. The scenery around me slowly melted into the twentieth century, and I would look down at the clothes I died in, my permanent wardrobe, and be reminded of how much I did not belong in that time.

Despite that feeling, it was invigorating to see other black men on television. The day CBS covered the March on Washington, one poor family in Newtown thought that their brand-new television was broken. No matter what they tried to do, the TV kept broadcasting "those negroes in Washington." I had hoped that they'd stay and watch, but finally they decided it was too nice an afternoon to stay inside and watch TV. Obviously, they were not sympathetic to those negroes in Washington or elsewhere for that matter.

Martin Luther King, Jr. inspired me as he did so many others. After so much bloodshed, including my own, his ideas of peaceful revolution felt like the purpose I'd been searching for all the time I'd walked the earth.

I often wonder if five years later, after his assassination, his soul walks the Lorraine Motel. Is he destined to be imprisoned in his own personal hell? Or did he get stuck in the hospital where his heart finally stopped beating? Was he lucky and did his soul get to rest for all the good he did in life? After all, he knew love, he knew compassion, and he was an instrument of peace. I hope he found peace in the afterlife too.

His death seemed like another letdown in a story of disappointments, but his dream stuck with me as it did with many others. Great strides were made over the next five decades. The situation improved, but hatred never seemed to lose its popularity. It survived, not only in the dark corners, but somehow it managed to thrive even in the light.

*

The first time I saw Lucy, she was walking out of a coffee shop with a fancy drink. I had heard other people leaving the café and raving about them. It had been so long since I tasted anything that dirt would probably be delicious to me.

Lucy was beautiful, no matter what coffee she drank. It was late August of 2018 when she started frequenting the café no more than three hundred feet from where I had died. She had brown hair, cut short, and blue eyes which could cut sharply. She was always well dressed in flowing skirts or fancy slacks and every day was a blouse of a new color. My favorite attribute of Lucy's was her smile.

I worked on all the terrible lines I'd use if I could talk to her.

*Someone better call the CDC 'cause that smile is infectious.*
or
*Are you tired? 'Cause you've been running through my mind all day.*

or my favorite

*I never had a number because I was born in the 1700s. Can I have yours?*

Who was I kidding though? I had a ghost of a chance with her. Also, she wasn't the type of woman who would fall for a line and I wasn't the type of guy to use one. People do stupid things when they fall in love, and believe it or not, I had fallen in love.

I had kept my promise never to venture out into the world on Halloween. I had become visible to a select few over the years for the purpose of scaring them, but since that first Halloween, I hadn't joined the corporeal world. My appearance mattered not to me all that time. Until Lucy.

I wanted nothing more than to talk to Lucy. Just a hello would suffice. My clothes would be hard to explain. It was a few months until Halloween, but I wanted to get close to her. I had to be careful not to bump into anyone. I could focus and touch objects or touch people, but I always left an icy feeling in my wake. If someone bumped into me, they would just go right through me.

I got awkward stares when I entered the café, but I headed straight for the cream and sugar counter and tried to look busy. It was a Tuesday, so Lucy would have ordered a plain coffee and would need to add cream. There is a fine line between stalking and admiring.

I saw her coming my way and realized it had been so long since I talked, I wasn't sure I could.

Then, she smiled at me. "Hi. You look like you've seen a ghost."

Laughter erupted, and it took me a moment to realize I was the volcano from which it spewed. "No, not today. I feel like I haven't slept in a couple centuries so I may be a little out of it." *Not a lie, nailed the lingo. This is going well.*

"That I can understand. I've been up all night grading papers." She was stirring in the cream, and I knew I didn't have much time left to chat with her.

"Oh, you're a teacher then?"

"Yep. First year here in Newtown. I am teaching freshman English."

"That must be a rewarding job." Over two hundred years with no one to talk to, and that's the best I could do.

"It is…sometimes." Her face lit up as she smiled again. "What do you do?"

"I, uh, I've done a little of this, a little of that. Some farming." I remembered my lie before rambling too much. "And, uh, I work at the historical society. I do reenactments. Hence the garb." I waited for her to call my bluff, but she responded with enthusiasm.

"Oh, that's amazing. I think the elementary schools send kids on the historical walks at the end of the school year."

"Yes. They do. This town is so rich in history. It's a great way for kids to learn when they find out it happened in their own backyard."

"I've learned so much since moving here. The first thing my landlord told me was that George Washington stayed here after the Battle of Trenton."

"That's true. He was a complex guy, you know. Brilliant mind for war. One time…" I caught myself before revealing my age. "Well, I don't want to bore you with more Washington facts."

"Oh, history is not boring at all! I do have to get to school though. Nice chatting with, um, I didn't catch your name."

"James. Barton."

She held her hand out to shake mine. "Lucy Anderson."

Her hand hung in open air waiting for mine, and I had to think quickly.

"I'm just getting over a nasty bug, sorry, I don't want you to catch it. But I am so pleased to meet you, Lucy."

"No worries." That smile. "Bye."

She walked out of the coffee shop, and for the first time, I wished I were alive.

Every Tuesday, I made sure I was in that coffee shop. Each week I was met with a smile and a new conversation. We talked about the weather. We talked about politics. We talked about her family. We talked about Yanny and Laurel. I was team Yanny; she was team Laurel. It seemed like that was the only thing we disagreed on in all our conversations. Every time I was with her brought me closer to believing my heart could beat once more. Each interaction was no more than thirty minutes, but no matter how brief, they were the best moments of my existence.

Tuesday, October 30 arrived, and it was time to be brave. Even rushing on to the battlefield had been nowhere near as nerve-wracking as asking Lucy on a date. The next day would be the only day I would be able to go anywhere other than State Street with her. More importantly, I didn't want to be the guy to give the term "ghosted" a whole new meaning.

I waited at the usual time that Tuesday, but she never showed. *Had something happened to her?* I spent the whole day worrying about her. I didn't even know where she lived and even if I did, I couldn't go there and check on her.

After pacing State Street for hours, I entered the clothing shop across the street from the café. I would be able to see if Lucy showed up from there and it was the first step in my plan.

The First National Bank & Trust clock struck midnight. The street was deserted, and I was the only soul still out at this hour. Even with no witnesses, it still felt weird to walk the earth in the flesh. I had been watching the clock from the clothing shop. I figured it would be easier to break into the store when I wouldn't actually have to break anything.

I had never shopped for clothing before, and I didn't

really know what would look good on me. After very little consideration, I decided to go with what the mannequin was wearing. I searched the racks and tried on a lot of sizes before finding the right fit. I looked in the mirror, and it took a moment to realize that I was the man staring back at me. I'd grown accustomed to my raggedy clothes. Even in life, I never really had a "Sunday best."

There I was in khakis and a blue sweater, and I looked like I belonged. It wasn't the clothes that made this man though; it was the will to live. I never had that either when I was alive.

I let myself out of the store and made my way to the library. I had been hiding spare change and small bills that I found around town under the tree just to the right of the entrance. I hoped I had enough in modern currency to show Lucy a good time. None of that mattered though if she didn't show for coffee. I knew what school she taught at, but that would be pretty creepy if I showed up there.

I carefully read the dates to make sure that the money was mostly current. After totaling it up, I had $68.26. In my day, that was a lot of money, but I had no clue what that could buy me now. I stuck it all in my pockets and headed to Carl Sedia Park. I had some time to kill it was nice to relax there or even take a stroll through the graveyard next to it.

I waited until the sun came up and then headed for the café. It was a little before seven when Lucy arrived. Instead of waiting for her by the creamers, I walked up next to her in line.

"Hey, I missed you. Yesterday, I mean." Her face looked grave, and immediately I thought I'd done something wrong. "Is everything okay?" The tiniest of smiles crept on her face.

"Yes. Thanks for asking. We had an incident at the school on Monday, and I was up late. I didn't feel much like stopping for coffee yesterday, and we had an early meeting."

"I am sorry to hear that. Was anyone hurt? At the school. It wasn't an attack or anything?"

"Physically everyone is fine. It wasn't an attack. Have you not seen the news?"

"No, I didn't catch it last night." *Because I was busy pacing the street worrying about you.*

"Well, we had some students write some racial slurs on the walls. It's so hard in the current political climate to keep our kids safe and to get the culprits to see what they've done is wrong. I just can't believe that in this day and age such discrimination still exists."

"I don't find it hard to believe at all."

Her face turned red, and she looked panicked. "I'm sorry. I didn't mean to offend. I guess you must have had your share of experiences with discrimination."

"You didn't offend me. I know what you were getting at, but I just know human nature and I've seen these actions again and again. When no one is held accountable, then nothing will ever change."

"I know it's not the same, but I get it. I mean I'm not a white male either." She smiled and I reciprocated.

"You know, that's one of the things I like about you."

"That I'm not a man?"

"Ha. Yes, I suppose that too. Also, you are so understanding and open minded. And I don't think you have an ounce of hate in you."

"Hate takes too much effort. Plus, what an awful way to live."

"I agree." I held her gaze just a little longer until a voice broke our trance.

"Can I help you?" We had reached the front of the line and the barista was ready to take our order. Lucy ordered a fancy coffee that sounded very sweet and creamy. "And for you, sir?"

I'd never been called "sir." I was so blown away that I forgot he was waiting for an answer. Not only that, I had no idea what to order. I went with the easiest answer and thought, *What the hell? I only live once a year.*

"I'll have what she's having. And I'm paying."

"James, you don't have to."

"Really, I want to. Not because I am a chauvinistic male, but I'm your friend and you've had a rough couple days. It's the least I can do."

"Well, I suppose that's sound reasoning. Thank you."

"My pleasure."

I paid the man, and we moved out of the way to wait for our coffee. I didn't know how long the drinks would take to make, but my window was closing and I had to act fast. We both started to speak at the same time.

"You first." She grabbed her drink off the counter and started sipping.

"Lucy, do you have plans this evening?"

"I do." My heart sank. "I'm going to dinner with you."

My heart soared.

"You could have killed me." *If I weren't already dead.* "Where would you like to go?"

"Dolce Carini. You know it?"

I didn't, but I'd be able to find it. "Yeah. What time?"

"Meet me there at five."

"Yes, ma'am."

"I've got to get to work, but I'll see you tonight." Her eyes lit up as she walked by me to get out the door. Just before she left, she looked back over her shoulder and said, "By the way, I like the historical garb, but you look even better in those clothes."

*Maybe they do make the man.*

*

I had little trouble finding the restaurant after stopping to ask for directions. The only problem was that I was still five hours early. I decided to find a sunny spot in the grass.

I spent a lot of time people-watching over the years, but the change of venue and the warmth of the sun on my skin brought me to a new class of observation. I was no longer watching people from the outside; I was one of them. I was breathing (more or less) the same air.

I completely lost track of time, but the sun changed position in the sky and clouds had moved in providing an unwanted cover from the light. I looked around for a clock but didn't see one. Just then, a truck with out-of-state license plates pulled into the parking lot. Three men got out and headed for the bar.

"Excuse me." I jogged towards the men. "Would one of you happen to have the time?"

They stopped in their tracks and one man turned around slowly. He glared at me, "Whatd'ya say, nigger?"

The smile ran away from my face, and I was transported back to a time I had tried so hard to forget.

The other men turned to back their leader as he started coming my way. I took a step back and braced for the beating that was sure to come. I'd been here before and knew it was best just to shut my mouth and take it. Maybe times had changed enough and a simple apology would help.

"I don't want any trouble. Sorry to bother you."

"Too late for that," the ringleader thrust the words out

through clenched teeth. "Someone oughta' send your black ass back to Africa."

I heard the blade exit the sheath before I saw it. My eyes grew wide, and his henchman looked around to make sure no one was watching. Times *had* changed; fists had become knives.

"You wanted to know what time it was? It's time for someone to put you in your place, boy."

"James!" The voice of an angel broke the tension.

The racist ringleader put the knife back in the sheath and spit at my feet.

"Let's get a beer." He took one last sneering look at me and then took the boys to their original destination.

I could see Lucy in front of the restaurant, which happened to be next to the bar. Worry covered her face. I kept my eyes on the men as I walked toward my saving grace. I had to make sure they didn't try to go after her or change their mind about that beer.

"Is everything okay?" she asked.

"Yeah, just poor timing. I guess." I did my best to reassure her, but the moment shook me and I had no clue how to comfort her when I felt no comfort. It didn't matter what happened to me, but I didn't want to put Lucy in danger. "You hungry?"

"Starving. I missed lunch today. You?"

"Feels like I haven't eaten in centuries."

*

We walked in, and the place was packed. There were little witches, superheroes, and villains. There I was, proud to be wearing clothes made in this century, but maybe I should have worn a cape. I was in costume, despite my normal appearance.

No one else could tell, but I knew.

"You wanna' split a pizza?" Lucy asked.

"That sounds good." I had already decided to let her do the ordering so I didn't make a fool of myself. Pizza didn't even exist when I was born. At least, not in the colonies. I remember reading that variations of it dated back to the Romans. I'd have to tell Lucy that when my nerves settled enough to get a coherent thought out of my mouth.

"Do you have a preference on toppings?"

"I'll eat whatever you choose." *I hoped.*

The waitress, Mandy, came over to introduce herself and filled up our glasses with water.

"Are you ready to order?"

"We'll split a large Hawaiian pizza."

"You got it." Mandy collected our menus and left us alone.

I took a look at the amazing woman across the table from me and felt pain in my chest. What was I doing? I'd spent so many years alone, and now I needed someone? More to the point, what if she really liked me? What was I doing to her? It's not like we could have a life. I had no life.

Even as these thoughts ran through my head, she looked at me, into me, and her face lit up as her eyes met mine. "Penny for your thoughts?"

I'd heard the expression. I knew what it meant. Still, I struggled to find the words to tell her. I couldn't very well tell her I was dead.

"I was…I was thinking about you." *Not a lie.* "I was wondering what made you want to come out with me tonight."

A somber look fell across her face. "You don't know?"

"Should I?"

"You should. You're not like other guys. You listen. You're kind. You're smart. You're cute."

My face got warm

"I figured, with those qualifications, I could give you a chance."

I knew I must have looked ridiculous at that point with the huge smile that was plastered on my face.

"Why did you want to ask me out?"

"Well, that's easy. You are the most amazing woman I have ever had the privilege to know."

"That's such a generalization."

"Oh, you want specifics? I'll be honest, your smile is what got me from the start. The more I got to know you though, I got to see how caring you are. I got to know your heart. You've got brains, looks, a sense of humor, but that pales in comparison to how beautiful your soul is."

She didn't break eye contact with me, and I couldn't tell if I upset her.

"So, my beauty pales in comparison?"

I panicked. "That's not what I meant."

I thought I had ruined the whole evening when she started laughing.

"I know what you meant. You are even cute when you're mortified. Thank you."

I breathed a sigh of relief as I went back to gazing at the amazing woman across the table.

*

Pizza was amazing! Food back in my day was no more than sustenance. At least, for people of my social stature. I could do without sweet coffee, but from that night on, I decided every

Halloween would be pizza night.

Lucy was also amazing! I wanted her to be in my life every day. Over dinner, she asked me about the men in the parking lot. I assured her that everything was fine and I'd dealt with worse. She got mad. Not at me, but I could tell that it really bothered her. She wanted to report the incident to the police.

"That's just not acceptable," she ranted. "It's 2018. You'd think that the days of hatred, racism, discrimination and utter stupidity would be over."

"It's fear, you know."

"What?"

"They are scared. I'm different, and that terrifies them."

"That seems like a blasé approach to a serious problem."

"I guess over the years, I've given up hope of change. I spent a long time fighting with no results."

"A long time? What are you, like twenty-five? You can't stop fighting until every asshole on this planet realizes it's not okay to hurt other people."

"I'm twenty-four." *Give or take a century or two.* "But I've seen a lot."

"Did you grow up in a rough neighborhood?"

"No. My personal experience was not as bad as others. But I tried to help those less fortunate than I was, and it never made much of a difference. It's like every time you think you've won something, you're just given this false sense of freedom. Something to tide you over so you don't realize you're right back where you started. The thing I've come to realize is that the light can't exist without the dark. Love and hate are mutual."

Her eyes looked so sad. "I don't believe you. I don't think you believe that either."

"What do you believe?"

"I think you're right to some extent. Dark and light, love and hate, none could exist without the other. But I know that love is stronger. I know the world seems more connected now with technology, but the truth is that it's more disjointed than ever. People have no qualms about sharing stupid bullshit on social media or arguing politics under the shroud of anonymity, but no one shares who they really are. If more people shared their differences, their stories, what makes them tick, then maybe that fear you talked about would go away. Maybe through our differences, we could realize we are all a little bit more alike than we think. You have to keep fighting even if the only change you see is small. Otherwise, the dark wins."

"Wow. I was right."

"Did you not listen to anything I was saying?"

"No, I was right about how beautiful your soul is."

*

We split the bill. She insisted since we mutually asked one another out in the first place. I not only wanted to appease her, but my afterlife savings wouldn't last too long and I didn't know where the rest of the night might bring us.

"There is a bookstore just down the way here. Do you want to go?" I didn't want the night to end, but that wasn't the only reason I agreed that sounded like a good plan. The promise of books was almost as great as the promise of more time with Lucy.

We walked in the shop, and it felt like I'd always imagined home should feel. The library was the closest thing I had to a home. The books, their smell, the knowledge that surrounded me were all a comfort that I'd never had before in life.

"I'm going to head back to the young adult section and see if I can find a copy of *The Hate U Give* for my classroom. I think after what happened the other day, some of my kids could stand to read it."

"Okay, I'm going to peruse the shelves up here." I meandered through the stacks. There was something different about the new book smell as opposed to the smell that filled the library's stacks. Both were equally comforting to me, but this one wasn't musty.

I saw a lot of titles that I had read. The library must have done a good job of keeping up with new releases. I was about to go find Lucy when an orange cover caught my attention. I picked it up and sat down in a bright red chair to read the jacket when Lucy came up behind me and peeked over my shoulder. I could feel the warmth of her breath on my neck as she said,

"That one's good."

For a moment, I forgot about the book in my hand as I breathed in Lucy's scent. I'd never been that close to her before, and I didn't want to move. Before I made the moment awkward, I turned to face her. "You've read it?"

"Yeah. It came out this summer, and it's not necessarily a beach read, but I plowed through it when I was on vacation with my parents."

"What's it about?"

"So much. I mean it's these people going to a powwow, but it says so much about Native American history and on the whole how they are so fractured. It's another story that those folks who fear differences should read."

"Well, on your recommendation, I'll have to get it."

I thought about stories I heard as a kid about the Lenape Indians. *They were savages. Worse than us negroes by far since they hadn't been tamed.* It wasn't until much later when I learned to read and started to understand a little more of history that I realized those "savages" were just trying to save their families and keep their homes. A little perspective goes a long way.

I saw the stack of books in Lucy's arms. "I see you got what you were looking for."

"And then some. It's a danger of visiting a bookstore."

"What would happen if we stayed longer?"

"Let's not find out tonight. I am working on a teacher's salary."

We both laughed and made our way to the counter with our purchases. Books in hand, we exited to the parking lot.

"Where did you park?"

"I walked." *Since the last vehicle I drove was a horse and carriage.*

"Really? Can I give you a ride home?"

*Home?* Not only did I not have one, but I really didn't want the evening to end.

"I live near the café, maybe you want to head there and grab a coffee before we call it a night?"

The smile on her face told me she didn't want the night end either. "Sure, I actually live around the block. You know, it's still really nice out. We could park the car at my place and walk to the café."

"That sounds great." I followed her to the car. I had never ridden in one before and didn't know what to expect.

I didn't doubt she was a good driver, but I was still terrified. I tried to hide my concern, but she looked over at me from the driver's seat and read me like a book.

"Are you scared of women drivers?"

"No, I just don't get into cars very often." I could tell by the inquisitive look on her face that was a strange response. "I was in an accident."

That wasn't a complete lie. I had been thrown from a speeding horse when I was younger.

"Well, I promise I'm a good driver. I'll keep my eyes on the road and off of you." Her smile reassured me, and I loosened up a bit. Her flirting didn't hurt either.

We made it safely to her house, and she parked out front on the street. I knew where we were and realized I had walked by her house millions of times. She lived close enough to my imprisoned radius, but that didn't mean I should keep seeing her. The ghost thing would be pretty difficult to explain.

For once, the world seemed right as my date and I walked in silence. The words that went unsaid were the most powerful. The café was growing ever near, and I didn't want that perfect moment to end, even though I knew it had to.

I dragged my feet a little, in the hope that she would follow suit. I kept my eyes wandering at the ground because I knew if I looked into hers, I'd have lost all restraint.

Fate took the liberty of stepping in on us. The wind picked up a little and brought a chill with it. Lucy walked a little closer and slid her hand in mine. The street was quiet, but our footsteps were barely audible over my beating heart. I had no clue how it was beating, but I recognized the sound and feeling from the first time I went to battle.

Lucy leaned in closer to me. Our shoulders touched. We could see the coffee shop ahead, but she stopped and turned to face me. She closed what little distance was left between us and wrapped her arm around my shoulder. With no protest from me, her lips were on mine. There I was, a 261-year-old man getting my first kiss. *It was worth the wait.*

We pulled apart, but my hand remained on her cheek. Her arms remained wrapped around me. That was the most perfect moment I'd ever experienced. Eternity wouldn't be half bad if it could be spent exactly like that.

*But moments are just that…moments.*

*

I knew something was wrong before I heard the roar of the engine. Lucy broke our connection, and bright lights blinded me. I didn't need to see though to identify the rattle of that truck and who was inside of it.

"Let's get to the café," I said keeping myself between Lucy and the truck. Doors slammed, and feet shuffled.

"Hey," a southern drawl called out. "You need some help, ma'am, or are you just a nigger lover?"

"Keep moving, Lucy. We don't want any trouble, sir." I figured bowing down to them might get us out of the situation.

But Lucy had other ideas.

"No, James." She pushed past me and charged the three racists. "You get the hell out of here, or I'll call the cops!"

"Blackie over here needs a girl to stand up for him," chimed in henchman number one.

"Maybe she needs a real man," called out henchman number two.

"Lucy, I know you think I am wrong, but let's go. This won't end well." But I could see the determination and fire in her eyes and knew my words were wasted.

"No, I'm calling the police." She pulled out her phone, and while she was looking down, the ringleader knocked it from her hands. I didn't take my eyes off Lucy, but I could hear the phone shatter on the pavement. She finally took a step back, and I finally took a step forward, putting myself once again between the men and Lucy.

"Don't touch her." My own fire was building now. I

knew they had weapons, at least I knew about the knife, but they were a threat to Lucy. "Leave and don't come back."

I had seen too many injustices in my time. I stood by for many of them without a fight. Lucy had been right earlier. I had nothing to fight for all these years, but she changed that. Standing by while crimes are committed is just as bad as committing them.

"I think you need to look at who you're talking to, boy. You ain't tellin' me what to do." The hatred poured out of him and I should have let it go, but I soaked it into my veins.

"You listen! Just take your cronies here and you get back in that truck and you get out of my town." I wasn't going to be bullied, I wasn't going to back down, and I wasn't going to let my voice go unnoticed.

He once again spit at my feet but turned around and motioned for the other two men to follow him back to the truck. For a brief moment, I thought I had won. The headlights still made it impossible to what was happening as they got in the truck. I hoped they were leaving, but I never pried my eyes away from their direction.

My hope was crushed as a shot rang out just as it had 237 years before on the same street. Truck doors slammed, and tires squealed on the pavement. Everything went dark.

*

The headlights were gone. The truck was gone. I looked down and saw a hole in my sweater. No blood. Hopefully it was dark enough that Lucy wouldn't notice, and I could tell her the bullet went astray.

I turned to make sure she was all right, but she was on the ground. I ran to her.

"Lucy!" Tears streamed down my face. "Lucy, hang on. It's okay."

I grabbed her in my arms, blood pouring from her chest. I had seen enough men die on the battlefield from similar wounds to know the situation didn't look good. I put my hand on her cheek, right where it had been moments before when she was warm and smiling. The heat I had felt then was quickly waning, and the smile that drew me to her to begin with was gone.

I heard sirens, but it was too late. I watched as the last light extinguished in her eyes. *The light cannot exist without the dark.* I kissed her forehead and laid her gently on the ground that was now stained with my blood and hers.

*

## <u>The Revolutionary</u>

*About: This blog was created to be the voice for those who no longer have one. The following stories are told from the perspective of victims of hate crimes. While liberties may have been taken in cases where the victim died, the author tries to remain as faithful to the facts as possible.*

*November 24, 2018*

*I have a nightmare. A shot rings out in the darkness. Another light has been snuffed out, and it tears my soul in two. I should hate them. The men who brought only darkness. I should hate them as much as they hate me, hate him, hate themselves. But where does that leave me? Alone, in the dark, and still dead as fuck.*

*It took some time to wrap my head around that. Being*

*dead. My parents always said I was so full of life. James said I had a beautiful soul. What do these things mean when nothing has meaning anymore? James told me it took him over two centuries to find meaning. I've never been very patient.*

*After my death, my parents started a non-profit that works to help stop bullying and provide safe places for those in need. I think of all the people they might save from similar fates. That means something.*

*After my death, the school I worked at started holding mandatory lectures on diversity and actually bought new textbooks so they could stop teaching history insinuating that slaves actually enjoyed their lives of servitude. That means something.*

*After my death, I got to spend every day with the love of my life. I got to see him for who he really is and the experiences he's had. I got to fall even more in love with him with each new discovery. That means something.*

*You took my life that night. But that's all you got. I still have the fight in me. I still have the hope that love is stronger than hate. I still have the will to make whatever change I can. I can find every sliver of light left in this world and help it shine bright enough to snuff out the hate and let love ring.*

*

The blog was Lucy's idea. Not even death can hold that woman down when she has her mind and heart set on a task. Within weeks, she had comments from people all over the world. They shared their stories and their light. We even thought some of the folks may have been deceased like us. *Ah, the wonders of modern technology.*

Every story gave us a purpose. Each a missing puzzle piece that helped bring the world a little closer together. Some found solace, some found hope, some found a cause of their own, but we all found each other. Lucy and I may have been invisible to the world, but we still had our voices and it was about time they were heard.

# Zombie Survival

Fog settled over the snow-covered landscape. The busy mob from the movie theater had dispersed, and we were the only two left on the road. Lights from a nearby stadium reflected off the water particles in the air, making everything bright. We had been walking in silence. Silence was what we existed in most of the time lately.

Kimberly's voice finally broke the tension between us. "So, did you like the movie?"

I nodded. "I loved it. I've always wanted to survive a zombie attack."

"It wasn't technically a zombie movie." Kimberly protested. "It was a movie about an outbreak that made people crazy. They weren't even zombies. They didn't eat people. They just killed them."

"Well, I know that," I replied. "It was kind of like a zombie movie though. Either way, it was a survival story, and I've always wanted to be put into a situation that is highly unlikely and then come out a hero."

"And what makes you think you would come out a hero, Tom? In the five years we have been together, the only thing I have seen you save is your money." Kimberly's flippant response caused me to stop walking.

"I just think it's smart to save our money for when we want to start a family. I'm not stingy, just practical. And about the hero thing, I will have you know that I have read the most prestigious books on how to survive zombie attacks and am an expert on the subject. I have the whole basement full of supplies in case the attack happens any time soon. And besides, I was born to be a hero." I put on a quick smile so she would know I was just kidding, but it was too late.

"Yeah right, sure." She scoffed.

With that, we were back to silence. The fog hadn't lifted in the least; in fact, it was getting harder to see. I started playing with my wedding ring, my usual nervous tic.

"We should have been home by now," she said. "I can't even see where we are." It was too late for the thought now, but she was thinking the same thing I was. We were lost.

"Yeah, we should, but why worry. It's a nice night for a walk. Other than the fog, it's not bad. It's warm." I was really trying to convince myself more than her, but it looked like I wasn't doing a good job of convincing either of us.

"Tom, I have to work in the morning. I just want to get home and get to sleep."

She put her head on my shoulder, not in an endearing way, but as a sign of how exhausted she was. She slipped her hand into mine and pulled me closer. The action was so jarring when I realized how long it had been since we'd actually touched.

"Look at me," she said.

I looked into her eyes. We held our gaze for the first time in a long time. I remembered as I looked into her deep hazel eyes why I fell in love with her in the first place. The fire I once saw in those eyes had burnt out, and I hadn't realized it. I struggled to find even a flicker of the former flame.

"I am sorry I have been kinda crazy lately," Kimberly said. "I know you are just trying to save us by taking time off from work and doing crazy romantic things, but we aren't in college anymore. We aren't kids anymore. We have real jobs. I am a doctor, and you are an architect. We aren't just playing make believe. This is real life."

I didn't know how to react.

"Say something." She pleaded.

I started to walk away from her, but she tightened her grasp on my hand and pulled me back. Her eyes were intense now, but there was still no spark.

"Kimberly." I waited a minute before I said anything I might regret. "Kimberly, what's the point of all work and no play? I fell in love with you because you had ambition, a heart full of passion. You wanted to get out in the world and live so badly. Do you remember when we went out in that storm? It was freshman year. The wind was blowing like crazy. I thought we were seriously in a hurricane, and there were trees falling all around us. The rain felt like shards of glass against our skin. Despite all that, we kept going. We walked all over campus and pretended like we were storm chasers. That was when I fell in love with you. Now, all we do is work. I feel like I am glued to my desk all the time, and you are never home. There is no adventure. That is what is wrong with us, baby. We just need some adventure."

Tears had built up in her eyes while I was talking. Those would surely extinguish any embers that could have remained smoldering.

"We are adults, Tom. We can't pretend anymore. *You* are an adult. You have an entire basement full of supplies for a zombie attack. Don't you think it is time to grow up?"

There was a clatter from behind us. Our heads snapped to the sound, and Kimberly wiped away the tears with the back of her sleeve. The fog hadn't lifted, and we were far away from the stadium lights at this point. I had no clue where we were and was worried the clatter may have come from a wild animal. There were no streetlights, at least none that were lit. I felt pavement under my feet and was pretty sure we were still on the road and not in the woods somewhere.

I grabbed Kimberly's hand tighter and pulled her behind me. I was ready to protect her from anything that might come our way.

"Hello?" I called to the noise.

There was another loud bang that sounded like it was on metal, then the sound of something rolling across the pavement. It was moving slowly, but it was moving towards us. "Is anyone there?"

I let go of Kimberly's hand and moved towards the noise. I crept towards the noise, waiting to see what would emerge from the fog. Then I saw the familiar silver metal that lines the curb every Tuesday morning. It was no more than a foot in front of me.

"It's just a trash can, no need to wo—"

*HISS!*

Out of the misty fog came a ferocious beast. I couldn't see what cut in front of me, but my face felt like it was on fire. Then, a cat landed softly on the pavement and ran back off into the fog.

Kimberly couldn't control her laughter. "Was that your zombie, sweetie?" Her voice was the most childlike I had heard it in a long time. "You were so brave. Now let's find our way home so we can get that scratch cleaned up. Look, I'm sorry, but there really is a time to grow up and stop believing in…"

Kimberly's face went white, her jaw dropped, and her eyes stared past me.

"In what? Zombies?" I asked.

She nodded.

"Okay, I get that. No more zombies."

She let out a scream and turned to run.

There was a woman behind me. She was drenched, and her face was pale. She stumbled closer and looked as if she had pulled herself out of a grave.

I ran after Kimberly and shouted,

"Kimberly! Stop!"

Fear washed over her face, and she had fallen to the ground. I gave her my hand and she reached for the lifeline.

"I'm sorry I didn't believe you. Please, we have to get away."

I turned again and looked at the woman, who on second glance through the clearing fog, it was easy to see she was alive and very dirty.

"Kimberly, she isn't a zombie. She isn't dead. She lives down the street from us. Stop freaking out."

Kimberly looked at me and then at the woman and back at me.

"You believe me?"

"I feel like a fool. I feel like... like..."

"A child?"

"Yes. I was truly scared of her."

"You were scared of me?" Our neighborhood zombie interjected. "With a headache and a sprained ankle, I hardly think you have to worry. I fell in a ditch over there looking for my cat because it was so foggy. Rascal likes it when it's foggy. I try to keep him inside, but he always finds new ways to escape."

"Rascal went that way." I pointed off into the bushes, which I realized were ours. "But I think you should see a doctor before you go off after Rascal. My wife is a doctor. She can call someone to take care of you."

I helped Kimberly off the ground, and she brushed some of the dirt off her clothes.

"Thank you so much. I'm Emily," the woman said.

"My name is Tom, and this is Kimberly." I shook Emily's hand and received a handful of dirt. Kimberly managed to escape with only a few crumbs, which she wiped on her already dirty pants and then pulled out her phone. She called the hospital as we walked toward the car in our driveway. I helped Emily in the back and then we drove to the hospital.

I pulled up to the emergency room door and got out to help Emily out of the car, but Kimberly was already on her way to assist.

"Thanks again so much, Kimberly," Emily said.

"You're welcome, Emily. And it's Kim. You can call me Kim."

I smiled as I watched the girl I married help Emily into the ER. She passed her off to another doctor, and when she came back to the car, I held the door open for her. She looked into my eyes and smiled. I closed the door and smiled even more. I could almost smell the smoke from the fire smoldering in her eyes.

# Emerald Aisle

*Keep busy*, thought Morgan. From her cubicle, she had the best view of her torturer. Slowly his hands ticked, leaving a fresh scar on Morgan's mind as they carried out their punishment. Only two hours to go until the vacation of a lifetime, and he chose now to move the slowest he ever had. These two hours would drag on forever if Morgan couldn't find something to keep her occupied.

In her excitement, she had been the most productive at work that she had ever been. In addition to finishing all her reports, she had also cleaned her desk and organized all the files anyone might need access to in her two-week absence. It wasn't often she took a vacation. In fact, the last time she was able to get away was just for a weekend three years ago. Her college roommate had a Vegas wedding, and while she was happy to leave the windy city for a while, the booze-filled weekend could hardly be called a vacation.

This would be different for Morgan. Not only was it going to give her a chance to relax, it would also allow her to cross something off her bucket list. Since she was a little girl, she had dreamed of traveling to Ireland. She longed to witness the Emerald Isle, and now, nothing would stop her from achieving her dream.

She had to look busy; otherwise her boss would find some project that would take her far longer than two hours to complete. She never used her work time to browse the internet, but at least it would look like she was doing something and she could do a little more reconnaissance on where she would be by that time tomorrow.

If she were at home, Ashford Castle would already be bookmarked on her browser, along with at least another dozen places she hoped to visit while she was in Ireland. Bookmarked or not though, it appeared her plan to waste time looking at pictures would have to wait. Instead of her home page, she was met with a "this page can't be displayed" notification. She typed in a few URLs and was met with the same response.

She stood up to check with Rose, who had the cubicle next to hers. Rose spent most of her day on Pinterest trying to find crafty ideas for things she would never create. If the internet were down for everyone, she would be the first to put in a call to IT.

Rose wasn't in her cubicle though. In fact, when Morgan looked around the office, none of her co-workers seemed to be there. She'd been so preoccupied that she hardly noticed the lack of usual noise. Even more unsettling, there was rarely a time when the phones weren't ringing throughout the room, and now with no one to answer them, not even one made a sound.

She picked up the receiver from Rose's desk and was met with silence. That had to be why Rose was gone. If she couldn't call IT, she would go down to the basement to get someone to fix the problem. *Where was everyone else though?* Morgan did need a distraction until she could clock out of work. Maybe if she took the stairs, it would eat up a little more of her time.

The heavy door echoed through the stairwell as it

slammed shut. The sound alone would have been enough to startle Morgan, but when the lights went out at the same time, the effect was terrifying. She was not one to let her emotions get the better of her, but in that moment, she could have been mistaken for the lead in a B-horror film.

She reached in her pocket for her cell phone to light the way but realized that she left it on her desk. She turned around to go back but when she pulled on the door, it didn't budge. She was locked in a stairwell, in the dark, all alone, with less than two hours until she was supposed to go on the trip of a lifetime. Her only hope was that she would be able to open a door on one of the other floors.

She shuffled to the wall and made her way to the top of the stairs. She grabbed the railing tightly and took a cautious step down, feeling for the step. It might take a while, but this wasn't as bad as she thought it would be. Just as she was getting the hang of it, she misjudged the distance between steps and before she knew it, she was tumbling down the stairs. She thought the stairs were bottomless and that she would never stop. Then, her head hit the wall.

-

*Slot machines chinked, and gamblers cheered as smoke mixed with the smell of booze and sweat. Morgan didn't see how anyone thought Vegas was a fun place to be. For some reason though, Vanessa and Phil decided that eloping was the better option. Morgan couldn't argue. She knew Vanessa's mother and had to agree that a wedding without her seemed to be the best option. She didn't think it would end well when her mother found out that the couple had eloped just to escape her wrath.*

*The big event was to take place at Charlie's Chapel of Love at 3:00 this afternoon. Vanessa and Phil had encouraged Morgan and Phil's best man, Lou, to enjoy the casinos on them while they spent the afternoon getting a jump on their honeymoon. Morgan had no intention of gambling when she agreed to the spontaneous adventure, but since she and Lou had each been given $50 to spend, it wasn't like she had anything to lose.*

*Lou was more than happy to spend his* per diem *as well. As soon as they hit the floor, he made his way to the blackjack table. With a $25 minimum, it seemed that Lou would be done with his $50 a little bit quicker. Always the conservative one with money, Morgan made her way to the penny slots. She had never gambled before and didn't really see the enjoyment in pulling a lever and losing money. However, it wasn't her money to lose to she settled in next to a petite woman in her 90s whose eyes were glued to the machine in front of her.*

*Not really knowing what to do, she put her money in, pushed some buttons, and pulled the lever. Waiting for bells and whistles, Morgan heard nothing.*

*"Max bet, honey." A raspy voice broke through the cacophony.*

*Morgan looked around and realized it must have come from the old woman next to her, even though her eyes were still glued to the slot machine. She looked from the woman to her machine. Sure enough, there was a button that read, "Max bet." The old woman said nothing else and Morgan figured she should take these few words as sage wisdom from a pro.*

*She hit the button and pulled the lever. The wise words did nothing for her. After repeating the process with the same results, she realized that her $50 was about to go as quickly as Lou's. Down to her*

*last dollar, she pulled the lever and stood. As she was about to turn
away, the machine erupted and lights flashed.*

*"I won?!" Expecting a couple bucks, Morgan was astonished to
see the word JACKPOT in bright lights.*

*"How much is the jackpot?" Hoping her slot buddy would
answer, Morgan turned to her for more help.*

*Without looking away from her own machine, she answered,
"Oh, that machine? It's only $10,000."*

*"$10,000!"*

-

Her head throbbed, and she thought she saw a sliver of
light, but it could have been that she was seeing stars. She tried
to get her bearings. *Vegas? Casino? Work?* That's right, she was at
work. It all came back to her a little too quickly, making her
head ache even more.

She felt around until her hand made contact with the
wall, and she used it to balance herself as she stood. As her head
cleared, she realized that there was in fact light coming from
beneath a door. She stuck her hands out and stumbled towards
it. She felt for handle and hoped that this door wasn't locked.

The handle gave no resistance, and slowly, she pulled the
door open. She expected to be blinded by the light from the
other side, but the room was dim. No overhead lights were on,
but the glow of monitors and the hum of electronics filled the
room instead.

She had been in the IT room when she was first hired and
given a tour of the building. It had been a few years, but she
remembered a room full of computer geeks and the constant
clacking of keys. She inched her way into the room in the dim

light where she could make out several workspaces and empty chairs, but other than the hum of computers and the ever-growing ringing in her ears, she didn't hear any human presence.

"Hello?"

Something clattered behind her, and she spun around quickly. With her head throbbing, she lost her balance and stumbled to her knees. She waited for a response and was not met with one.

She waited for the dizziness to subside a little and then pulled herself up to the nearest workspace. The computer monitor was on, but the screen was black with only a blinking cursor. She picked up the phone next to the monitor.

*Silence.*

Where was everyone? Had there been a fire alarm? Was the building evacuated?

Something was clearly wrong. Morgan decided she had to get out of the building. Whatever was happening, it wouldn't do her any good to stay in there alone and in the dark.

She carefully turned back to the door when static broke through the silence, causing her to jump. She looked around the desk and didn't see anything that could be making the noise. A garbled voice came through the white noise, "…landing… minutes… winds from the west…"

Morgan had a moment of *déjà vu* but was too busy opening the drawers of the desk to find the source of the noise. She reached the bottom right drawer, and there on a stack of files was a handheld radio. She felt for the talk button and hoped in the dark that she was pressing the right one.

"Hello? Can anyone hear me?"

*Static.*

"What is going on? Is anyone out there?"

*Static.*

She thought the signal must be terrible in the basement. She had to get to higher ground, and then maybe someone could hear her. She clipped the radio to her belt and went back the way she came.

Her head felt like it was in a vice grip. The lack of light made her even dizzier as she navigated the treacherous twenty feet from desk to door. A real sense of worry kicked in now that she was alone, injured, and had to navigate the stairwell in the dark. On top of all that, she was concerned she wouldn't get out of there in time to make her flight. She had a hatred of airports, and it wouldn't make it any easier if she had to run to catch her flight. She swallowed her worry and opened the door.

-

*"What happens in Vegas, ssstays in Vegas, baby!"*

*"Well, Lou, I can assure you that is one thing that will not be happening in Vegas."*

*Vanessa and Phil had said their I Dos and Lou had proceeded to drink enough for the happy couple, Morgan, and himself combined. He now hung on Morgan's arm as she helped him to his room. He seemed to think that this meant Morgan would be staying the night in his room.*

*"I can't believe you won all that money." His words slurred and he stumbled into the wall, pulling Morgan with him. "You ssshould use some of it to get the hotel to fix thisss hallway. It's like walking in a funhouse."*

*"That's not the hallway, Lou. That's your eyes. Let's just get you to your room, and you can sleep it off." She struggled to pull him*

back upright and keep him balanced while getting him the last ten feet to his door. "Lean on the wall while I get your door open." It was good that she had the foresight to ask for his room key after the first five drinks. He thought she was asking for another reason.

Morgan was always the one taking care of others. Cleaning up their messes. Keeping the unruly ones in line. It started with her father who fell apart when her mother left. Someone had to make sure he would wake up for work every morning. Someone had to make sure the bills got paid. Morgan knew that her tight rein on life was her coping mechanism for getting over being abandoned by her mother. Unlike most kids who have a parent walk out on them, she never dreamed of her mom walking back into their lives. On the contrary, she hoped that her mother never would. What could she possibly say that would make up for abandoning a child?

The lock turned green, and Morgan took one step inside to hold the door open. "Okay, Lou, get into bed, and I'll get you some water."

"Do you wanna' take my clothes off, or should I?"

"How about you wait until I leave, and you can have the honors."

"Oh, I get it. You are going to go downstairs and sseee if you can win sssome more. Okay, I'll wait up for ya."

"Okay, Lou. You do that." She filled up a cup of water from the bathroom sink and set it on his nightstand. "Just drink this and get into bed." She set his room key down next to the glass and headed back for the door.

"Good luck!" Lou called.

Morgan's response was muffled by the closing of the door.

She stood in front of the elevator. Her room was two floors up, but she didn't feel tired. Her flight was at seven the next morning, and *the smart thing to do would be to get some sleep. She never let loose though, and maybe Lou was right,* What happens in Vegas stays in Vegas. *Morgan hit the down arrow and decided to celebrate her friend's wedding and her winnings with a nightcap.*

*It was 2 A.M., but the bar was still bustling with patrons. She found an empty seat between a middle-aged woman in a sparkly red dress and a man around her age wearing a tuxedo. He made her think of James Bond so when the bartender asked what she was drinking, a vodka martini seemed like the only choice.*

*The drink was strong. She only had a glass of champagne earlier, and the last time she drank anything other than a beer was in college. Deep down, she knew why she sat there. She wanted to talk to the man in the tuxedo. She definitely needed liquid courage for that. She pulled the olive out of her glass and downed what was left. Setting the glass back down, she turned to the man to her right.*

*"Hi." She smiled and even as she was doing it, knew that she looked and sounded absolutely pathetic.*

*"Hi." Bond, James Bond replied then stood up abruptly and walked back toward the casino.*

*Defeated, Morgan placed a twenty on the bar and said,*

*"Keep the change"—she got off her stool and muttered under her breath—"ya filthy animal." She and her father's love for the movie* Home Alone *led them to say that every time they left a restaurant and the tradition stuck with her even after her father died.*

*She headed back up to her room and thought that three hours of sleep sounded better than none.*

-

Morgan was plunged back into the dark. She felt for the radio to make sure it was still clipped to her belt. It was her safety net in these trying times. She didn't think about it the last time she was in the stairwell, but now she wondered why the backup security lights hadn't come on like they should when there is a power outage.

Her priority was to get to higher ground, not wonder about the lights. She felt her way along the cool wall until she reached the stairs. She grabbed the railing and started working her way up to the top. She could waste her time trying doors all the way up or just keep going up all fifteen floors and hoping that the door to the roof was unlocked. She knew that the best signal would come from the roof and decided that was her best option.

She ignored the headache and focused on placing her feet securely on each step. It was eerie how her footsteps echoed through the empty stairwell. She didn't believe that she wouldn't have noticed everyone else evacuating the building, but maybe her dream of Ireland was more consuming than she thought. It must be possible to drown out the surrounding world. She did it before when she came back from Vegas. She remembered the trip, but it seemed to her like one second she was in Vegas and the next she was back at work. The trip back was a big blur to her. She always attributed that to the dread of returning to her monotonous life. But that wasn't a dream that was all-consuming; that was a nightmare.

Out of breath, she reached the last set of stairs. She crossed her fingers and checked her belt again to make sure the radio was still there. She reached out for the door handle and let out a sigh of relief when the handle turned and the door opened.

*The door opened, and the woman in the sparkly red dress from the bar was standing in front of Morgan.*

*Morgan had just been settling into bed when there was a knock at the door. She thought it must be Lou, trying to make good on his promises to bed her. She didn't expect this stranger.*

*"Morgan?" the lady in red asked.*

*"Yes. How do you know my name?"*

*"I think we know each other."*

*"I don't think so, ma'am."*

*"I heard you. At the bar. 'Keep the change, ya filthy animal.'"*

*"Um, yeah. I said that. But I still don't know you."*

*"Why did you say that?"*

*"Look, it's late. Or early. I have a flight to catch. Whatever you think, or whoever you think I am, you're wrong. Sorry." Morgan tried to close the door, but the woman stuck her foot in and blocked it from closing.*

*"Please. Just hear me out, and if you think I am crazy, I will leave you alone."*

*"I do think you are crazy, and I will call hotel security if you don't leave right now." Morgan struggled with the door, and the woman pushed back.*

*"Your father's name is Martin," the woman rambled quickly. "You were born February 29, 1976, and your mother's name is Janice."*

*Morgan stopped trying to close the door.*

*"My name is Janice."*

*Morgan took a step back and let the woman in the room. Words couldn't find their way into her mouth, but it hung open as if something might escape. The woman cautiously took steps towards her until Morgan held her hand up motioning her to stop.*

*"No, this isn't right."*

-

"No, this isn't right."

It should have been light outside, but as soon as Morgan opened the door to the roof, she realized it was nighttime. Even more jarring was that she could see the stars. None of the other buildings were lit up, and for the first time since she lived in the city, she could see the entire night sky.

She grabbed the radio from her belt and pushed the button to talk, "Hello, is anyone there? This is Morgan O'Reilly, and I need help."

She held the radio close to her ear so that she would be able to hear a response over the wind. Nothing came out of the radio. The wind was heavy in her ears, and panic was heavy in her body. She clung to the radio, her silent lifeline, and pressed the talk button again.

"Hello? Please, if anyone can hear me, tell me what's going on. This is crazy."

-

*"This is crazy. You are crazy. You're not my mother."*

*"I am, Morgan. I could tell you how sorry I am, but I know words will make no difference. I just thought…I just thought it must be fate that all these years have gone by and I found you."*

*Morgan stared in disbelief.*

*"Do you want me to leave?"*

*"Yes."*

*Janice turned around in defeat.*

But as she put her hand on the door, Morgan said, "Wait! Why?"

"Why what?"

"Why did you leave us?"

"I fell in love. I met a man. He asked me to go back to Ireland with him. He got a job at Ashford Castle, and we were just so in love and I fell in love with the country. And it's not that I didn't love you. I just couldn't stop myself. I was so unhappy with your father and—"

"Stop. Just stop. I don't care if you're telling the truth or not. Just leave." Janice moved back towards Morgan and held out her hand.

"Morgan, I..."

Morgan batted her hand away.

"Get out! Get out! Get out!"

Janice and Morgan were both crying, and Janice made one more attempt to make contact with Morgan. Frenzied, Morgan shoved her back, and Janice lost her footing. She fell hard into the table and knocked its contents to the floor as she followed behind them. Blood quickly pooled around her head on the beige carpet. Morgan bent over her and grabbed her shoulder. Janice didn't respond. She shook her hard and called her name, but still, she got no response.

The whole incident was surreal. Morgan knew she wasn't dreaming as the metallic scent of blood filled her nostrils. She knew the right thing to do was to call the police. It was an accident. Every part of her that had held it together all these years unraveled in seconds. She felt the tears streaming down her cheeks. Her heart raced. Absolute panic took over her composed demeanor. She knew what was right, and still she threw on the clothes she had set out, shoved her pajamas and last-minute belongings into her bag, and called a cab to take her to the airport.

She stepped around the cooling corpse of Janice, and without *even a glance back, she left the hotel room she had briefly inhabited and prayed that what happened in Vegas would truly stay in Vegas.*

*Morgan had no recollection of the cab ride to the airport. She went through the motions, including tipping the cab driver $100. What did she care? She had $10,000 to spend. She went through security, expecting at any moment that someone would pull her aside and slap the cuffs on her. Almost disappointingly, she made it through with no problems. She found her terminal and an empty seat which she occupied numbly for an hour until they started boarding.*

*She didn't even remember getting on the plane, but there she sat in her aisle seat, feeling her ears fill with pressure as the plane left McCarran Airport. Reality started to creep back in as the flight attendants made their way through the aisles with snack carts.*

*"Would you like anything, ma'am?"*

*Morgan stared blankly ahead and calmly replied, "Water, please."*

*The flight attendant let the tray down and placed a napkin in front of Morgan. He poured her a cup of water, and as he placed it on the napkin, the plane hit a little turbulence and he spilled on the tray. Water trickled off into Morgan's lap.*

*"So sorry, ma'am. Here are a few extra napkins." He looked back at the lavatory. "The restroom is available if you need to clean up at all."*

*Morgan didn't respond to the water in her lap or the man's apologies.*

*He waited a moment more, and when Morgan didn't say anything, he asked, "Are you all right?"*

*"Yes."*

*Before she could elaborate, a voice came on the radio.*

A voice came on the radio.

"Captain…experiencing….hold tight…be…Chicago soon." The static made it hard to decipher anything the voice said, but Morgan was ecstatic hearing another human being.

She pushed the talk button, "I am so glad to hear you! Can you repeat that?"

The city around her was still so dark and the wind was chilling her to the bone, but just knowing she had made a connection started to warm her. The static cleared a little and she heard more the second time.

"This is Captain Arden … experiencing … turbulence … hold tight, and we'll be landing…Chicago soon."

*Turbulence? Landing?*

Somehow Morgan was picking up feed from an airplane. She looked up in the sky, but the only objects above were stars. She couldn't believe she would be able to pick up something like that, especially if the plane wasn't in the sky above her. All the warmth she had been feeling seconds before escaped her body.

*Turbulence?*

-

*"…turbulence. If you all just hold tight and keep your seat belts fastened, we'll be landing in Chicago soon."*

*The captain seemed calm as he spoke through the garbled speakers, but the passengers around Morgan were less than calm. The bumpy plane ride had quickly turned from a little turbulence to a frightening experience. The overhead lights flickered, and the air flow in the cabin seemed to have come to a stop. The chatter from other passengers went from murmurs to harsh whispers as Morgan sat still, oblivious to what was happening around her.*

*The captain came on the speakers again. "Folks, the winds seem to be a little greater than we predicted. A storm popped up that wasn't on our radar. We aren't going to be able to land at the moment, so just bear with us as we get out of this rough patch."*

*The plane was now being thrown so violently up and down that Morgan emerged from her trance. She looked around to see the panicked faces of the other passengers, but panic entered her face as she realized that all of those faces looked like Janice. Guilt was setting in, and in the back of Morgan's mind, she knew there was nothing she could do to redeem herself.*

*A flash of light outside the windows lit up the cabin, and the whole plane leaned to the left as smoke filled the already stale air. Screams erupted, and wind and rain blew through the cabin. The passenger next to Morgan was holding on to her arm and reciting the Lord's Prayer.*

*"That's not going to help you," Morgan said to her neighbor. The words were lost in the cacophony of nature now whipping through the aisles. Morgan unbuckled her seatbelt, unlatched the hands around her arm, and pulled herself into the aisle. Grabbing the sides of seats, she started to make her way to the lavatory.*

*She stumbled and almost lost her grip a few times along the way, but she made it to the lavatory, yanked the door open, and threw herself inside. It was still loud, but the difference in the noise was deafening. She gripped the tiny counter space on the sink and raised her eyes to look in the mirror where she had the best view of her torturer.*

# Melody

I was at PuttPutt Town on the main street downtown. It was my usual hangout spot in the summer. I had been going there since I was ten, and I was now twenty-three. My first time there I went with my brother and was amazed at the small course of eighteen holes that wrapped around the small piece of land between a Starbucks and a bar. Nothing says family fun like mini golf, coffee, and alcohol.

Unfortunately for my brother, I had never mini-golfed before, and I thought the method used to drive a ball was the method used to mini golf. One bump on the head later, we became friends with Melody, the beautiful girl who worked there, and I returned every day in the summer.

She was four years older, but she never treated me like just a kid. She didn't even tease me too much about smacking my brother in the head. When it was slow, she'd even join me on the greens and completely slaughter me. I never cared what the score was, just spending time with her felt like a hole-in-one.

That day, the sky was cloudy and, in the distance, extremely dark. Being situated on a lake, the town was prone to summer thunderstorms, and one was definitely waiting to strike that day. The thunder rolled in the distance, and soon PuttPutt would be closing up the doors for a short break while the storm passed through and drenched the greens.

"Business is bad this year. It's been raining too much. Who wants to play mini golf in the rain?" Melody asked while hanging her head out the service window. "Not to mention you are still between jobs, so I get no money from my best customer."

"Well, if I had money, I'd play in the rain. It's the damn lightning that's scaring people away." I stepped out from under the awning to see if the rain had started to fall. The sun had gone away, and there was no way the rain would miss us now.

"Hey, you know if you stopped spending money in that bar over there, you would have money to golf," she said in her sarcastic tone that urged me to change my ways.

"I am just supporting the local economy, and it's technically field research for getting the brewery up and running."

"Uh huh. If that's the case, make sure you keep your receipts so that you can deduct your drinking habit from your taxes."

"What a great idea! I knew there was a reason I liked you." My attempts to flirt seemed futile.

"Oh, I am full of great ideas. In fact, you wanna help me close up the case with the putters and windows too? I have a feeling no one is gonna come right now anyway."

"Do I get paid?"

"I might be able to spare a pop for you while we wait out the storm. But don't ask for a raise."

"Well, I'll take the job. It's the best offer I've had in a while."

I reached up to grab the flap, and a swarm of bees flew down darting at my head. I ran away like a little girl and narrowly escaped the wrath of what seemed like a thousand yellow-and-black hellhounds.

When I finally felt it was safe, I took my hands away from my head and heard Melody laughing and gasping for air. She was doubled over and could not control herself. She looked up at me, and her knees were red from where she had been holding them. Not only did I lose my manhood with that act, but it hurt more that she was going to the police academy in a month. Real danger awaited her selfless sacrifice.

*So much for my attempt to ask Mel out today.*

Not that I would have really asked her out since I hadn't asked her in the thirteen years I had been going there. My brother had asked her out once, or so he said. He said she was too busy; I think she said no.

Mel was finally settling down, but tears had formed in her eyes from laughing so hard.

"Hey now," I said, "It wasn't that funny. Besides, bees are scary."

"Yeah, Joel, are you allergic?"

"No, but that doesn't mean anything. They still hurt if they sting you."

Mel walked towards me and pinched my arm.

"Ow!"

"Just as I thought, you are a wuss. Haha." She turned to finish closing up, and I went to chase after her but was interrupted by a blood curdling scream. I had never heard anything like that in my entire life.

"What the hell was that?" I asked.

We bolted around the building to get a view of the street.

"Oh my God, Joel, look!"

The thunder rumbled, and then all was silent as a car rolled down the hill with the passenger side door open and a woman being dragged along beside it. I was frozen. I didn't know what to do. All I could think of was my life. It was as if I was the one being dragged beside the car and my life was flashing before my eyes.

*I was seven. My brother, Nathan and I had a neighbor who liked to capture squirrels and kill them. His whole backyard was full of the cages he captured them in, and the tool shed had all sorts of blades and poisons depending on his choice of murder for the day. Nathan and I thought we had the perfect plan, as most adventurous children do. We waited and watched for weeks. Or maybe Nathan waited and watched. Regardless, the time came when all the cages were full and we knew that he was going to kill them that afternoon. After some convincing, Nathan got me to skip school with him, and we went to the fence. I hoisted him up over, and he quickly opened all the cages, letting our furry friends loose on the asshole's garden. I shouted in excitement, and Nathan quickly motioned for me to be quiet. After he made sure the squirrels got away, he came back to the fence. The one flaw in our plan was that we didn't think about how to get my brother back over the fence.*

*"Joel," Nathan whispered, "you have to go get the ladder from the garage and put it over the fence."*

*"I can't. I can't reach it."*

*"You have to try. I can't get back over."*

*"I can't. You have to find another way."*

*"Just go try. Try!" His voice was more frantic now. All of a sudden, I heard a door open on the other side of the fence. "Joel, he's here, help me." With that Nathan ran away from the fence, and I ran to school. I didn't want to get in trouble.*

*He had stayed hidden in the tree until the neighbor went back in his house. His plan worked until he tried to get down from the tree on our side of the fence and broke his leg. Dad still doesn't know that I was there too.*


I was twenty-three. A car was screeching down the hill, and the sound returned. People were yelling, and the rain was starting to come down in big drops. A man from the top of the hill was running behind the car, but he would never catch up to it at this point. The woman being dragged by the car didn't make a sound, and other than the bumps and potholes on the road that caused her to bounce, she didn't move. Her car wasn't slowing down at all and wouldn't on this hill without some kind of intervention.

Every inch of me wanted to turn and run, to pretend like I had never seen any of this. If I didn't see it, maybe it didn't really happen. But just as I turned, I saw Melody. She was throwing off her flip flops so that she could run after the car. I was frozen until I saw her.

She shouted, "Call 911, Joel!"

As she ran by me, I caught her arm.

"Wait, I'm wearing shoes." I started towards my bike and yelled back at her as I took off. "You will never catch the car on foot. You call 911!"

Empowered, I pedaled as fast as I could to try to catch up with the car. I didn't have a plan for how I would actually stop it when I caught up to it, but I was determined to do something this time.

I was right behind the car, and the rain was coming down in sheets at this point. I could barely see the woman so I couldn't tell if she was all right. The car seemed to be slowing, so I pulled to the side to try to free the woman. I reached out and could feel the fabric of her shirt. I reached a little farther and then my bike stopped abruptly. I flew through the air right before everything went black.

I felt sick. I tried to open my eyes, but they seemed like they were glued together. My mouth was dry, and everything hurt. I cracked my eyes and saw my dad and my brother. Melody was in the corner and had a bandage around her forearm. I was in a white room. I didn't recognize it, and I didn't remember what had happened. I opened my mouth to talk, but my throat was dry and scratchy and no sounds formed.

"Don't try to talk, Joel." I recognized my dad's voice. "You hit a car while you were on your bike. You are pretty banged up, but you will be fine." So much for saving a life, and I am sure I looked very stupid in the process.

Melody stepped closer to the bed and said, "If it makes you feel any better the woman in the car is alright. I know you didn't save her, but you made a valiant effort."

"Yeah, right up until he slammed into a bright yellow car," my lovely brother interjected.

"Your arm?" Each word was a struggle as it left my lips.

"Oh, it's fine. Don't worry" Mel replied.

"It's not fine," Nathan said. "She burned it saving that woman's life and then had to pull your sorry ass out from underneath your bike and pull you out of the road. My brother would get saved by a girl."

"Enough," my dad said in a stern voice.

"And you wondered why I said no, Nathan." Mel looked at him with disdain.

"Nathan," my dad said, "let's leave them alone. Joel needs to get rest anyway."

Nathan looked at Mel, and realization washed over his face. He probably realized what he lost when she said no.

"Don't pay attention to Nathan," Mel said as the door closed.

"I don't anymore." My voice was returning. "I am sorry about your arm."

"Don't be, just a little burn. Dudes dig scars, you know. Besides it's not your fault. You know what? I am proud of you. You know what else?"

"What?"

"I didn't just say no because Nathan is an ass. I was waiting."

"Waiting for what?"

"You." I was dumbfounded. I didn't know what to say. I smiled because things were looking up for the first time in my life. She looked at me with her beautiful blue eyes and winked.

She walked to the door and turned before she left. "Don't keep me waiting."

# Not My Type

I was walking by this thrift store that operated out of a garage on Decatur when it caught my eye. The metallic sheen, the smooth keys, and the aged paper fed through the beast all screamed to my tortured soul. On the yellowed paper, two words were typed:

BUY ME

So I did.

The owner of the store told me he didn't have any paperwork on the typewriter, but he figured it was probably from the '60s. I hoped that like the gun, this Remington would make a bold statement.

My agent was hounding me for the next great thriller and constantly reminding me I was under contract. As if I needed a reminder. The bills stacked on my desk were suitable enough as the last of my advance leaked out of the bank account.

Everyone read *Cut the Cord*. Everyone knew my name. No one knew that despite the millions of copies sold worldwide, I was still nothing more than a destitute writer.

A destitute writer with writer's block.

I never believed in writer's block. Doesn't matter if you don't believe. Tell that to the climate change naysayers.

Each day my deadline grew near. I knew all about dead

lines; those were all I wrote. What made matters worse was that even if I managed to write something worth selling, my debt wasn't about to go away anytime soon. I owed money to people who don't send bills. They send messages.

After my wife died, I'd started gambling. I had beginner's luck and kept going until the luck ran dry. I'd always judged addicts until I found myself offering up the same lines.

*I'll stop. This is the last time. Just one more time won't hurt. I don't have a problem.*

I did though. It wasn't that it filled the hole Adelle left in my life. To be honest, the hole had always been there. Gambling filled the time, and cards filled my head with thoughts that weren't of her voice, her body, her light.

I needed that light more than ever. Darkness had followed me from childhood, but she kept it at bay. Without her by my side, it wasn't a matter of if I could go on, but how I would go on with my life.

When I got home from the thrift store, I cleared my desk by shoving all the paperwork to the floor. A cluttered floor was better than a cluttered desk. I set the typewriter down and stood back to see how it looked. Who knew if it would help the writing process, but hell, it made my desk look good. I grabbed a fresh sheet of paper from the printer and fed it though with ease. The pure white space was a worse tease than the blinking cursor.

I thought it best to take it for a test drive with a poem I had written for Adelle.

A summer eve,
a winter day,
October brisk,
breath of May.

Ocean blue,
but burning red,
your eyes on fire,
with words unsaid.

My heart to yours
and yours to mine,
weathering the seasons
has never been so divine.

The keys felt right against my fingers, but it could have just been the familiarity of the words that kept her alive in my mind and in my heart. Tears rolled down my cheeks. Spontaneous leakage of tear ducts was common those days. I pulled the sheet of paper out of the typewriter and stuck it in my drawer.

I fed another clean sheet through and positioned my hands on the keys. I am sure I looked like some pianist ready to begin a magnum opus composed hundreds of years ago, but my blank stare at the blank paper was probably more reminiscent of John Cage's *4'33"*.

*Cut the Cord* was a psychological thriller about a child who suffered under the rule of his helicopter parents until he took matters into his own hands. It was so easy to write. Follow the formula: one unreliable narrator, multiple unlikable characters, then insert psycho/sociopath here. The next book should have just been rinse and repeat. That's what the fans wanted and what the publisher wanted.

But it wasn't what I wanted. I wanted to write something that had meaning. Those days, meaning didn't sell; murder did.

My thoughts were interrupted by clacking. I looked down and realized I'd been typing. I had a whole paragraph in front of me, but I didn't remember anything that I had written.

> She was strangled, that much was clear. Deep ligature marks on her neck suggested the weapon was heavy and thick like a rope or a cable. A struggle was apparent by the blood under her fingernails and the objects scattered around the living room. If the attacker was in the system, this would be a pretty easy case to close.

Well, it wasn't the worst thing I'd ever written. Maybe it could go somewhere. It lacked substance, but maybe it would be another creation of cheap thrills to please the masses. If I could settle my debts, maybe I could relax enough to write something of worth to the soul and not the wallet.

I looked up at the clock and was shocked that it was already 7:00 P.M. Somehow, I'd been sitting at my desk for over two hours. In those two hours, I'd typed one measly paragraph. I had to get out and get some fresh air.

All the ways I tried to take my mind off Adelle and I still made it a point to head over to Lakeshore Drive and plop my ass on our bench looking out over Lake Pontchartrain. We met at University of New Orleans when I was working on my M.F.A.

in creative writing and she was working on hers in film production. Whenever we needed to clear our heads, we would head down to the lake and look out to endless possibilities. That was the one place I could still feel her spirit and be at peace.

The sun was setting, and I closed my eyes. The beauty of being a writer, failed or otherwise, was that my imagination lacked nothing. I could conjure up the scent of her soap, lavender and vanilla. I could feel her hand in mine. She always joked my hands were too big and I joked that hers were too small, but somehow, they fit perfectly together. I could feel the weight of her head on my shoulder. A weight I gladly welcomed. And I could fall asleep on a public bench with the heart-wrenching hope that all that was real.

I woke to *Tequila Sunrise* playing from my clock radio. I was in my own bed. Feelings of lying next to Adelle lingered, but as I climbed out of my slumber, reality hit hard. My head ached almost as much as my heart that morning. I had no recollection of how I got home or why my head hurt that much.

I stumbled to the bathroom and took a good look at the dark circles under my eyes. *No visible damage, so was liquor the culprit?* I needed coffee.

I brushed my teeth, ran a comb through my short, black hair, and threw on mostly clean clothes. It was a five-minute walk to Café Gentilly. I had hoped the fresh air would jog some memory of last night, but I was still puzzled when I pulled open the door to the café.

I went there often enough, and the routine was always

the same. I set a ten on the counter, got a cup for coffee, waved to Steve who was slaving over the stove, and headed over to the counter to fix my coffee. After the first sip, I found a seat and waited for my breakfast.

It was slow at the moment, so my breakfast came with a side of Steve. "How's it going, Tori?"

"Been better, been worse."

"Who hasn't? How's the writin'?"

"Making progress. I might have two paragraphs by this time next year."

"Well, if ya ever need to take your mind off things, we could always use help translating for folks seeking asylum. You'd pick up plenty of stories that need telling there too."

"Steve, you know I'd feel like I was exploiting them. But, if I feel up to it, I'll stop by sometime." My eye caught the television hanging high on the wall behind Steve. "Hey, can you turn up the volume?"

"If I could find the remote." He got up to look for it, but the news story I was interested in was already ending. The news crawler at the bottom of the screen had a snippet of the story and it read: Garden District Woman Found Strangled in Her Living Room.

I reached in my pocket for my phone to look up the story but felt only the cold metal of my keys against my fingers. I was of the perfect age that I knew what it was like to exist without the constant connection but still felt the pang of withdrawal not having the world at my fingertips.

In my hurry to get caffeine, I must have left it at home. I scarfed down my eggs and hash browns, refilled my coffee to go, thanked Steve, and headed straight home.

I slid my new typewriter to the corner of the desk and booted up the laptop. Bordering on frantic, I typed in:

*murder garden district new orleans march 19 2019*

Stories popped up from every local news source and even a couple from national networks. A picture of the house must have been the only suitable one to use. It looked familiar, but I'd walked through the neighborhood enough, I'd probably seen it in my many travels.

Authorities weren't releasing any names, but it looked like a break-in leading to murder of opportunity. Then, I read the lines that stopped my heart.

> *The twenty-seven-year-old victim was strangled with a tieback from the curtains. Police say she did fight back and are hoping to have leads later today from DNA evidence found under her nails.*

I glanced from the computer screen to the paper jutting out of the typewriter. Obviously there were some similarities, but even I had the thought yesterday that my measly paragraph was nothing earth-shattering. It was the start of a terrible crime novel that was so generic it was almost as if it were ripped from the daily police log. If I were to glean anything from that pure coincidence, it was that I should go back to the drawing board.

I fed the paper out of the typewriter, crinkled it satisfyingly into a ball, and chucked it into the waste barrel beside my desk. I leaned back in the chair and closed my eyes. I felt the warmth of the day oozing into the house from the open kitchen window.

Adelle and I always argued about the temperature. She couldn't stand extremes. But me, I loved to soak up the heat. My body never felt warm enough except when I was in her arms. Sometimes, on extremely humid days, I would sit at my desk with piping hot coffee, clad in a sweatshirt, and as the sweat poured out of me, so did the words. That seemingly excruciating process was my comfort zone. I made my own personal hell fires to expel my demons. Now, the demons didn't want to be expelled.

I had to get out of the house. I knew I wouldn't be able to write, so I figured I could make good on a promise instead. The bookshop in the Garden District had asked me to stop in and sign fresh stock of my book. I may not have been Anne Rice, but in the wake of Gillian Flynn, *Cut the Cord* sold well enough for my local store to keep it on the shelves.

I found my phone on the nightstand and slid it in my pocket. I closed the kitchen window and locked the door behind me. As I unlocked my car door, I reassured myself that I was really going to fulfill a promise and not because the bookstore happened to be near the scene of the crime.

Fortune was on my side. I found a spot on St. Charles. It was a convenient walking distance to the bookstore and even more conveniently positioned two blocks from a house surrounded by crime scene tape.

It was still a little early to go to the bookshop so I pointed my feet towards the scene of the crime. There were only a couple police cars at the scene, but they had the sidewalk in front of the house blocked off as well. I wasn't the only onlooker hoping to catch a glimpse of something gruesome. A crowd had gathered across the street, and tourists and locals alike snapped shots of a rather dull crime scene.

Most likely, the body had been removed at that point. The lack of action didn't stop the mob from hoping to catch a macabre thrill. That's not why I was there. In some corner, the far-reaches of my mind, there was something a little too familiar about the whole thing.

Maybe my subconscious knew more than I thought. Maybe that's why I had typed that paragraph yesterday. Maybe I was a desperate writer who was reading far too much into a tragic incident.

I decided abruptly to brush the whole thing off as a coincidence. I started to double back to the bookshop when I saw the car in the driveway. It was a pink Audi A3 Cabriolet with a license plate that read: DRAMAQN. I knew who drove it.

Emma and Adelle dated before Adelle and I did. In the break-up, Emma lived up to her license plate. I hadn't seen her in years, and I was grateful for that.

Of all the ways she could find her way back into my life, this had to be one of the worst ones. Not knowing if she was the victim or if she'd walk out the door and see me, I decided I'd spent enough time gawking and set off for the bookstore.

I loved setting foot anywhere books were sold or

circulated. Bookstores were one of the only places I still felt like myself. I'd like to think it was the cozy feeling, but honestly, I think I was happy to be surrounded by stories that weren't my own.

The clerk saw me walk in and had the books for me to sign setting on the counter. I was grateful she busied herself with a customer so I didn't have to make small talk. I was still trying to wrap my head around recent events. I am not even sure if I signed my name or just wrote gibberish in the blank space above my printed name.

I snuck out after I finished defacing a dozen title pages and headed downstairs for coffee. While I waited, I noticed two police officers outside the café. It was absurd to think that they knew I had any connection to the murder around the corner, but their presence made me uncomfortable all the same.

I grabbed my coffee, headed out the door, and quickly walked back to my car and the sounds of clanging bells from the streetcars on St. Charles.

I had every intention of writing when I got home, but the couch was calling my name. When I awoke to the sound of clacking, I didn't know how long I'd been asleep. That disorienting effect of disturbed sleep washed over me, and for a moment, I felt like I wasn't alone.

When clarity finally arrived for me, I listened hard to hear the sound that jostled me awake. I heard a drip from the faucet, the faint shrieks of children playing outside, but no clacking.

I dragged myself off the couch and grabbed a water from the fridge. Adelle would have made me place a coaster under it, but her absence meant my desk would have another water ring. I plopped myself into the chair and slid the typewriter in front of me. I was determined to write something and not let the day go to waste. As I moved the carriage right, I realized I already had.

```
        I watched her take her last breath.
The eyes truly are the gateway to the
soul, and I could clearly see hers leave
her body.
        She begged. I didn't know people
actually did that. I thought for sure,
if I could catch a fleeting glance of
her soul, she should be able to look me
in the eye and see the evil that resided
within my soul.
        I must have hidden it well since
she thought she had a chance. Evil in
plain sight is the most dangerous of
all.
```

Twice now, I had typed out dark storylines with no recollection of doing so. As far as I could remember, I hadn't been drinking. I didn't feel drunk. A quick glance at my phone showed I'd only fallen asleep for an hour. While I was in a fog when I woke up, the sound of keys clacking was vivid in my mind. That could mean two things: I was losing my mind, or someone was in my house.

I rummaged through my bottom drawer until I laid a hand on the Glock I kept but never had any intention to use. I checked the clip and pulled back the slide.

I took a moment to listen again and was met with silence. I made my way room by room through the shotgun house. Nothing seemed out of place, and I didn't find any evidence that someone had been in my home. My palm grew sweaty against the handle of the gun. Then, sweat broke out on my forehead as I looked up at the kitchen window and saw that it was open.

I'd closed it before I left the house earlier, and I didn't remember opening it when I came home. I was beginning to feel like one of those unreliable narrators losing her mind. I ran to the back door and found it locked securely. I headed back towards the front door and found it in the same state. Things weren't looking good for my sanity.

I rested my head against the door and closed my eyes. I never pictured myself as the hopeless, pathetic woman who couldn't cope without her wife. But there I was, just that. I was always under the assumption that Adelle and I had a partnership, but it was quite clear now that she had always carried the brunt of not only her baggage, but mine as well.

*BAM! BAM! BAM!*

The door pounded against my head. It was a good thing I didn't keep my finger on the trigger; otherwise, I would have had a hole in my foot. I quickly shoved the gun in the kitchen drawer and opened the door just a crack.

"Hi, ma'am, I'm Detective Glapion, and this is Detective Manx. We're with the New Orleans Police Department." She and her partner flashed their badges. "Are you Victoria Keller?"

I opened the door all the way.

"Yes, but you can't use your badge to get an autograph." I chuckled nervously, but the detectives didn't join me.

Obviously, they weren't big readers. "Just a little author humor."

Manx realized who I was. "Oh, you're *that* Tori Keller. Loved the book! When is the next one coming out?"

"Workin' on it." I offered a faint smile. Glapion still didn't know who I was, or maybe she didn't care. Whatever led them to my door was probably something more nefarious than seeking an autograph. "So, what can I do for you?"

"Do you know Eileen Mount?" Glapion asked.

"Yeah, she's my agent." Not the question I'd been expecting, but once the confusion passed, I realized I had a meeting scheduled with her earlier in the day. A meeting that I missed due to cruising a crime scene and sleeping on the couch. "Shit! Did she call you guys just because I missed our appointment?"

"So you weren't at her office around noon today?" Manx asked.

"Nope."

"Care to let us know where you were?" Glapion was not impressed with my terse response.

"Asleep. On my couch. Look, I know it's rude to miss an appointment, but is a police presence really necessary?"

Manx and Glapion looked at one another and Glapion, obviously in charge, offered a subtle nod to her partner.

"I'm sorry to have to tell you this, but Eileen is dead." Manx did his best to look sympathetic, but I could tell he hadn't done many notifications.

"Well," I paused long enough to consider if my thought

should be spoken out loud and decided I couldn't help myself. "I guess she won't be mad at me for missing our meeting."

Just like the autograph joke, this one fell flat as well.

"I take it you weren't close?" Glapion stated coldly.

"Not really. Don't get me wrong. I am not happy she is dead, but we had a business relationship, nothing more."

The detectives' stares seared through me.

"You wouldn't know of anyone then who might want her dead?" Manx broke the silence.

"I mean, doesn't everyone have at least one person who wants them dead?"

"Do you have a name for us?" Glapion was clearly annoyed.

"No."

"Well, thanks for your lack of help Mrs. Keller. If you think you might be able to help us, give me a call." Glapion handed me her card, turned abruptly, and headed back to their car, leaving Manx standing on my porch like an uncomfortable prom date. He nodded at me and turned to leave.

But I stopped him. "Can I ask how she died?"

"She was strangled. Bare handed. Got a handprint clear as day on her throat. Seemed personal. Have a good day, ma'am."

I let him go this time and closed and locked the door behind him. I staggered back to the typewriter and stared at the words that had begun to haunt me.

In true addict fashion, I headed down to the casino on Canal. Why not squander what little money I had and ignore my already shattered life that seemed keen on continuing to break?

Let it Ride was what I needed. I didn't have the energy to read other players, and I certainly didn't want the small talk. I didn't have to think, and all I needed was dumb luck. I tried to focus on the cards, but my mind kept drifting to the dead bodies piling up in my periphery. I kept telling myself, *It's not a pattern until it's three.* Maybe I was as callous as Glapion assumed.

I looked down at my chips. Somehow, I'd lost most of them already, and it didn't seem like I'd been sitting there that long. I was down to $36. I laid the chips out for the next hand. I wasn't playing to win at this point, and it felt like I'd lost my taste for the vice. I wasn't even a good addict anymore.

I didn't look at my cards, but I placed them under the first pile of chips, letting the dealer know to let it ride. He flipped the first card to reveal the ten of spades. I slid the cards under the last pile of chips. He flipped the second card. It was the ace of spades. He pulled my cards out and flipped them. Others at the table clapped, and the dealer congratulated me. I finally looked at my hand and realized I had a royal flush. I did the math for what I had bet.

I just won over $50,000.

The addict in me should have said to keep going, but Adelle's voice came through loud and clear.

"Take the money and run, dumbass."

I followed part of her advice. I cashed in my chips and bought a case in the gift shop. My winnings wouldn't pay all my debts, but it would get the loan shark off my back for a while. *Think of the devil.*

Eddie the loan shark was waiting for me as I gave my

ticket to the valet. "Where y'at, Tori? I see you have something for me."

"I see your spies are out in full force, Eddie."

"Not spies. Think of dem as bodyguards. I have to protect my assets after all."

"Is that all I am to you, Eddie?"

"Well, you're a great *asset*." He grinned chauvinistically while checking out my ass.

"And you never fail to prove you're an *ass*hole."

"Now, Tori, is that any way to talk to someone you still owe a shit-ton of money to?"

"Look, I'll talk to you any way I please. You'll get your money, but I don't need your bullshit." I shoved the case of my recent winnings into his arms as the valet brought me my keys.

"I only let you talk to me that way, Tori, because you're not a real gambler!" Eddie shouted after me.

"I only talk to you that way, Eddie, because you deserve it!" I stopped before getting in the car. "If I'm not a real gambler, what am I?"

"A lost soul. Adieu!"

I didn't feel like going home. My encounter with Eddie had my skin crawling, and home was not a comforting place those days. I headed to Prime Example, a jazz club not far from home. A stiff drink, some good music, and delicious gumbo might make the day end on a better note.

About half way through the first set and half way through my second Sazerac, a woman caught my eye. I didn't know if it was the warmth of the booze or the fact that she was absolutely gorgeous, but the room felt like it was on fire.

I hadn't even thought of being with anyone since Adelle died, but there I was staring into a set of eyes that stared right back at mine. I grabbed my drink and made my way to those sultry, dark eyes. Her skin was midnight, and I wanted nothing more than to feel it on mine and get lost in the night.

"I'm Tori." The rasp of desire in my voice didn't even surprise me.

"Serafine."

"Can I buy you a drink?"

"No." Her body moved towards mine like a wave crashing to shore. "But you can take me home."

*Clack, clack, clack.*

My head throbbed. Maybe Sazerac was a bad idea. I was full of those lately.

I was in my bedroom. I couldn't remember much of what happened the night before, but I knew I had brought Serafine home with me. *Had she left?*

It was dark in the room, which was probably a good thing for my head. I stumbled to open the curtains, and the sudden light made my head throb. I closed my eyes and blindly searched for the tieback. I couldn't find it, but when I opened my eyes, I saw that my hands were stained red. I looked back at the bed and saw the sheets were stained as well.

I rushed to the bed and lifted the sheets. I caught a whiff of sickly-sweet red wine and it all rushed back to me. Serafine did come back to the house. We opened a bottle of wine, but I was already beyond drunk at that point. We carried on like awkward teenagers until I knocked the bottle over and thoroughly doused the flames of desire. She got a Lyft home.

Despite the disastrous night and the painful morning, I felt more like myself than I had in a long time. Maybe I had finally hit rock bottom and was working my way back to the top.

I collected all the stained linens and garments and threw them in the trash. There was no point in trying to salvage them. I cleaned myself up and then padded down the hallway to the kitchen to make some coffee. I flipped on the television and turned to the news while I waited for the coffee to brew.

*Police have identified the victim as Edward Boudreaux. Boudreaux was known to authorities for being involved in several illegal activities although charges were never brought. It's too soon to say if any of those activities may have played a role in his death.*

I shut the TV off and fell into the couch. Eddie made three. The coffee pot gurgled from the kitchen, and I got up to pour a cup. I missed the first part of the story so I went to my desk to pull it up on my computer. As I opened the laptop, I saw the fresh writing blossoming from the typewriter.

```
    It's said that alligators can
survive at least a year, maybe more,
without eating. They not only store
their energy, but have a way of using as
little as possible. Their ability to
survive and persevere sure makes being
cold-blooded rather appealing.
```

A human can bleed to death in
seconds or weeks, depending on the
wound. Severing an artery is a sure way
to put you closer to seconds. Panic
makes your heart beat faster. It pumps
the blood out double time.
    An alligator chomping on your leg
will probably make you panic. With a
bite strength of over two thousand
pounds per square inch, there isn't much
you can do but crawl away as he munches
on the leg that used to be attached to
you.
    That's a loan Eddie won't be
getting back.

I shoved the typewriter off my desk, and pieces scattered across the floor. Hot coffee burned my hand as I forcefully set the mug on my desk. I grabbed the computer and typed in *edward boudreaux* and clicked on the first news story.

*The remains of Edward Boudreaux were found in the swamps this morning by a tour group. Members of the group say they heard someone calling for help, but by the time they reached his body, Mr. Boudreaux was dead. Boudreaux's leg was severed. Authorities are pursuing all avenues of inquiry, but at the moment, they are unable to determine if this unfortunate end was due to malicious intent or tragic accident.*

Eddie was dead, and I had the story of his death typed out on my floor. I checked the locks, the windows, and every room. I was alone, and the only logical explanation was that I'd gone mad. *I might as well turn myself in to the police and confess.* I glanced over the broken typewriter and took a deep breath. That's when I saw it.

I'd lived in New Orleans my whole life, and I knew a *gris gris* bag when I saw one. The tourist shops were filled with them, but those shops were just out to make a buck. This bag looked old. This bag looked legitimate. I was no expert on voodoo, but as crazy as it sounded to me, magic was a better explanation than the only logical one I had.

The typewriter had to be cursed. There was no way I could have killed three people and remembered nothing. I picked up the bag and examined it.

*Knock, knock!*

"Shit! Better not be the cops." With the bag in hand, I opened the door. It was Serafine.

"Hi, awkward, but I think I dropped my phone in your car last night."

"I drove last night? What a fuckin' idiot."

"Yeah, I think we both made some stupid decisions."

"Look…"

Serafine held up her hand to stop me. "No apologies. Really, we were both impulsive and drunk, and you obviously have some issues to handle."

"Still, I don't do things like that. Not that I am insinuating you do…"

"Tori," she interrupted. "Best stop while you're still above ground." She was smiling, but the events of last night were still a little fuzzy. I wondered how big of a fool I had been.

"Let me grab my keys."

"Wait." She grabbed my arm. "Is that a *gris gris* bag?"

"Yeah, I think. I found it in my typewriter. Do you practice?"

"Why? Cause I'm black?"

"What!? No, I was just...just..."

"Relax, I'm fuckin' wit' ya. My granmè dabbled and taught me a thing or two. That bag in your hand looks like bad news."

"Like 'I shouldn't be touching it' bad news?"

"It probably should have stayed hidden. Has anything weird happened?"

"Define weird." This shit was getting weird.

"Okay, look, that symbol stitched into the fabric, it's Hecate's Wheel. Whatever this bag was meant to do, probably has to do with spirits. Seen any ghosts lately?"

"I haven't *seen* any."

"You're probably okay. I'd take it to someone who knows how to get rid of it though. Best not to mess around with it."

"So granmè didn't tell you how to get rid of them?"

"No, never on the lesson plan. But I can make you a mean luck bag if you got some lodestone."

"I could've used that about eight months ago. Let me get my keys." I clicked the fob and shouted out to her, "It's open!"

"Can you give it a call?" She shouted her number to me, and I dialed it as I walked to join her at the car. By the time I reached her, it was ringing in her hand.

"You found it."

"I already had it when I asked you to call it. I just wanted you to have my number in case you work through those issues." Her smile was enlightening.

I chuckled. "I certainly have quite a few of those. I appreciate it, Serafine, but I don't know that things would work out for us."

"Ah, you're only into black girls for one-night stands?"

"You're fuckin' with me again, right?" I asked. She nodded and smiled. "I just don't have a lot to offer."

"Eh, that's okay. Skinny white girls aren't really my type."

"Yeah, yeah, you're not my type at all. But maybe I'll see you around." I flashed her a smile.

As she walked back to her car, she called out, "Maybe."

And maybe one day, I'd have something to offer.

I closed the car door and turned to go back inside when I saw a silver case in the backseat. It looked an awful lot like the one I had shoved into Eddie's arms. I opened the back door and grabbed the case. Not only was it the same, but it now had blood on the handle.

I picked it up and looked suspiciously up and down the street since that was the normal thing to do in the situation. I closed the car door, locked it, and booked it back to the house. I put the case on the floor and leaned on the kitchen counter. *So much for any moment of clarity or relief.*

I saw Detective Glapion's card on the counter. I had to call her. Regardless of what was going on, I was involved somehow. My brain couldn't put the pieces together, but maybe hers could. I pulled my phone out to dial and realized I wasn't alone.

"Babe, who are you calling?"

I couldn't see my face, but I felt all the blood drain out of it.

"Adelle?" I turned slowly to face my dream and my nightmare all rolled into one.

"Miss me?" That smile once lit my soul on fire, but this time, it left me cold. Her bright eyes were full of something, but life was not it. Her auburn hair flowed, once lost not from battling the disease, but battling something far worse than the disease——the cure. The woman before me was not my wife, but that didn't stop my heart from wanting her to be.

"So much. How?" The words left my mouth in exhales. "How are you here?"

"You needed me. But then again, you always have, darling."

"But you're dead. How are you here? Am I imagining this?"

She started walking towards me, and I stiffened.

"Relax." She reached out and touched my face.

I closed my eyes. It felt like her touch, her hand. She smelled like spring flowers.

"It's really me. 'A summer eve, a winter day, October brisk, breath of May.' My poem, you typed me to life."

I opened my eyes wide. Her hand was still on my cheek, and she closed the distance between us with a kiss. She felt the same, but it was like coming home after being robbed.

I gently pushed her away and started to pace. "You can't be here. It's not natural."

A hearty laugh escaped her mouth.

"Neither is being gay, according to some, dear. It's like I said, you need me. You're floundering, but I'll take care of things. I already have been." The dark realization hit me.

"Emma? Eileen? Eddie? You did that? Why?"

"Emma? She was a practice run. I've wanted to kill her since we broke up, and to be honest, it was rather fun. Eileen? She's been robbing you blind and sucking your soul for years. I told you that you needed a new agent, and now you can get one. And Eddie? If you don't know why on that one, I can't explain it to you."

The whole experience was surreal, but I listened in a stupor.

"I did it all for you."

"For me?" I exploded. "The police are already asking questions. How do you know they won't accuse me of everything? I've got a bloody briefcase full of cash that—"

"That *you* won last night."

"And then gave to a dead loan shark in front of casino that probably has cameras to capture the act. Hell, I'm probably the last person to see him alive!"

"Relax, you aren't. I am. You worry too much. There is no evidence to tie any of these things to you. And if any ties to me, legally I am dead. You can't arrest a dead person."

"This is New Orleans. I wouldn't be so sure of that."

"Stop pacing! It's annoying."

I stopped but kept my distance. "I love you, Adelle. I do. But this is wrong. All of it is wrong. You shouldn't be here." I started pacing again. "I'm fuckin' crazy. *This* is crazy."

"You want me to be dead? Me? Your wife. I've been cleaning up your messes for years, and this is how you treat me?"

It's been said one should never piss off a redhead. One should really never piss off a dead redhead.

She started throwing anything she could get her hands on, and I managed to avoid most of the dangerous items as I ran for the bedroom. I had left the gun in the nightstand after pulling it out yesterday. Adelle felt like she was flesh and blood so I hoped a bullet might stop her.

I yanked open the drawer and felt for the gun while keeping my eyes on the doorway.

"Babe, have you always thought me an idiot?" Her voice rang from the hall.

"You're not an idiot," I stalled when I realized the gun wasn't there.

Adelle appeared in the doorway with the gun in hand. "You almost shot your foot off yesterday. I couldn't just leave this lying around."

The woman I loved would never have shot me, but this Adelle, she was not the woman I loved. But, she thought she was.

I changed my attitude. "Smart thinking, gorgeous. You are always lookin' out for me."

"Someone has to." Dead or alive, Adelle wasn't gullible.

I had to tread carefully. "I just need to wrap my head around this all. It's a good thing, you being back. You get to stay, right? This isn't a temporary thing?"

"You know, I don't know. I guess we can find out together."

"I'd like that." I slowly got up and made my way to her. "You need to tell me everything. Why don't I make some tea? I mean, you can drink, right?"

"Of course I can drink."

I could see an anger rising again in her. "Obviously, but I am new to this whole necromancy thing. You'll have to forgive any stupid questions I may have. You know I said dumb shit before all this."

She laughed, almost cackled. "Yeah, you sure did. How about when you were talking to those cops yesterday?"

I inched past her towards the kitchen, and she grabbed my hand. It felt so good. It fit perfectly just like it used to. "You heard that? Not my best moment."

"Let me make the tea."

"No, no, you relax. You've been doing so much for me."

She looked at me suspiciously but acquiesced. She took her place on the couch, folding her right leg under like always and placing the gun on the table.

I saw the *gris gris* bag on the counter. I didn't know if reanimated Adelle had any superpowers, so I had to hope my legerdemain would be enough to conceal my plan.

I checked the kettle for water and repositioned it so it would block the bag that I placed on the burner next to it. I flipped the knob, turning on the burner with the bag. I had never longed for a gas range until now, but I had to make do until the electric stovetop warmed. I wasn't even sure if burning the bag would do anything, but it was the only opportunity that had presented itself.

I turned back to face Adelle, hoping my slender frame would be enough to block the stove. "So, what have you been up to since you died and came back to life?"

"That's what you want to know?" she asked incredulously.

"Well, is it all murder, or do you stop for coffee on the way?"

"Maybe pick up girls in bars you mean?"

"Oh, that. Are you jealous? To be fair, I thought you were dead."

"I'm not jealous." She got up from the couch and seductively walked towards me. "In fact, maybe you should invite her over. She is quite sexy."

I put my hands on her face to keep her from peering over my shoulder. "That should go well. 'Hey, Sera, my dead wife, brought back to life by voodoo, thinks you're swell. Wanna' have a little *ménage à trois* this afternoon?'"

"I see your sarcasm remains fully intact in the mourning process, dear. I—" She started to choke on her words, and her skin felt very hot on my hands. She shoved me off her as I tried to kiss her. "What did you do!?"

Adelle pushed me to the floor with more strength than she ever had while alive. She ran to the smoking *gris gris* bag and threw it towards the kitchen sink. She was smoking, in every literal and figurative sense of the word.

Unable to get up quickly enough, I inched away from her and tried to get to the gun with my feet kicking frantically. I was not fast enough though, and with lightning speed, she was picking me up by the shirt. Her face was inches from mine, and I started to sweat from the heat emanating from her.

"You always liked it hot as hell, babe. Now you can join me there!" The words came through gritted teeth with an anger I'd never felt from the woman who brought so much light into my life.

I saw more smoke behind her as the alarm went off, and I realized the bag must have caught the curtains when she threw it. Flame burst from the fabric, and the kitchen quickly turned into an inferno.

I tried to loosen her grip on me and succeeded miserably when she threw me against the wall. Blood trickled down the side of my face. I tried to push myself up against the wall, but Adelle was right there. Her skin glowed as red as her auburn hair. She grabbed me by the throat, and her hand burned into my skin.

"Do you know how many people would kill for a second chance? You ruined that!"

"I wouldn't kill for one. I was happy with the first chance." The words left my mouth in a whisper as I struggled to breathe.

Adelle started to scream, but her voice disappeared into the roar of the flame. I collapsed to the floor, free from her grip. Smoke mangled my lungs, and I felt the urge to close my eyes and sleep.

Keeping low to the ground, I tried to crawl to the back door. I only made it a few feet when my body gave up and my face hit the floor.

Through the narrow space between my eyelids, I thought I saw Adelle's hair blowing in the flames. Delusional or not, I felt her soul smile before my eyes closed and gentle darkness comforted me like my wife's embrace.

"Will someone stop that damn beeping!?" Scratchy and raw, I barely recognized my own voice.

"You'd have to die to do that," a voice replied. It was familiar but one I couldn't place it until I opened my eyes and saw Detective Glapion standing by the bed.

I was in a hospital, and the torturous heart monitor proved I had survived the unbelievable events of the past week. How? I wasn't sure. Maybe I had dreamed the whole thing in some drug-induced haze. No matter the truth, the detective was here for answers that I wouldn't be able to give.

"You're pretty lucky to be alive." She must have read the confusion on my face. "An off-duty firefighter was not far from your house, and she had a scanner on in her car. Do you remember how the house caught fire?"

"It's all kind of fuzzy." My voice cracked, and I motioned to the water pitcher on the table. Glapion poured me a cup and slid the table within my reach.

"Witnesses say that they heard an argument before the flames broke out. Was someone else in the house with you?"

"Did you find evidence of that?"

"Answer the question," the annoyed detective urged.

"No." Even if I said yes, there was no way I could explain Adelle.

"That burn on your neck sure looks like a handprint." I reached for my throat and felt gauze. "We got a picture from the E.R. doc."

"Are you one of those folks who can see Jesus in toast too?"

"Funny." She didn't laugh. "The fact that witnesses heard two voices and that you have an interesting burn would lead us to believe that someone was there with you."

"Hey, you must be a detective. Look, I don't really remember. If you say someone was there, maybe they were."

"Hmm, do you take anything seriously, Mrs. Keller? You almost died, your house is ash, and I have the feeling you know a lot more than you're letting on. If you're protecting someone, now is the time to think about the consequences you'll face."

"Detective, I am not protecting anyone. I can honestly tell you I don't know a single living soul who would do these things. I'm sorry I can't be of help."

Glapion narrowed her eyes, trying to get a read on my veracity. Either she believed me or just knew she wouldn't get anything further from me.

"All right, Mrs. Keller. I hope you're back on your feet soon." She left her card on the table. "I am sure the last one I left you burned up…in the trash."

I thought I saw a faint smile crack at the corner of her mouth.

"Hey, writer's inquisitiveness, can I ask you something?"

"Sure."

"I assume you compared the handprint on my neck to Eileen's since she was strangled."

"Yes."

"Did they match?"

"No. The print on your neck was made by a smaller hand."

"Hmm, thanks." Glapion stared me down a bit longer. "Good luck with the case." She nodded and walked out the door as Serafine entered.

"What are you doing here?" I asked.

"Is that a question you ask the woman who saved your life?"

"You saved me? The detective said a firefighter pulled me out of the house."

"And women can't be firefighters?" Her look told me to stop digging.

"Never said that. Just didn't know you were a firefighter."

"Yeah, I suppose we had other fiery topics to cover other than my career when we met."

"Probably for the best. I would have made the evening more awkward by saying something like, 'Your smile sets me ablaze' or 'You're smokin'' or…"

"Stop, stop, stop! You didn't go there. Please stop. Don't tell me you think you're a comedienne?"

"Writer."

"Worse."

"Absolutely." The banter was the most joy I'd had in my life in a long time. "I should take you out to dinner sometime."

"To thank me for saving your life?"

"Among other reasons."

"I thought I wasn't your type."

"Yeah, probably not. But I think that's a good thing."

In 2012, a fantastic feline by the name of

Emilita Isabella María Santina Anna Pinta
Guadalupe Dominga Rodríguez Sanchez
Scroogè Siders de las Botas

found her way into my life.

At this point, she is far more famous than
I and for good reason. While she had
assistance with typing, the following
story is one of her own creation,
completed between naps.

# The Rat
## by Emilita

I could feel his beady eyes watching my every move. Here he was, some piece of vermin thinking he could outwit me. I was not only the biggest cat in town but the most dangerous, and if there was one thing I absolutely did not tolerate, it was a rat.

I should have known not to trust this guy from day one. Thing is, around here, we look out for our own kind. It was surprising enough, I suppose, that he was willing to give up his family that easily, but times were rough for everyone and he kept food on the table for us. Or rather, under the table.

That night though, I was on the prowl.

"Al? I know you're in here." My voice wailed through the abandoned shed. It may have seemed like I was the only one in here, but I knew all of Al's hiding places. There was no hole in the wall in this town that he could hide in which I wouldn't be able to find him. He must have known this when he decided to betray me. Without me, he never would have made any cheese. He would have been living a life of constant fear in absolute squalor. Well, he might have enjoyed that last part.

*Clink, Clink!*

I turned quickly and got really low with my weapons drawn. I would have given anything to sink my claws into him at that moment. Then I saw him as he scurried behind some boxes. I quietly positioned myself so there was no chance for him to escape. I had him cornered now. This felt like old times.

It was not long ago when we first met and were in the same position. I was about to go in for the kill when I heard this little pipsqueak.

"Wait, I can help you," he sobbed. I stopped myself just in time.

"Carry on then, how can you help *me?*" I replied.

"I can tell you where everyone you are looking for is hiding. Where they live. When they will be there. Everything. Please, just spare my life."

And so began the unlikely partnership that would now end just as it had started. Here we were again, and this time I would not be so understanding.

"Any last words, Rat?"

"Please, just kill me. I am tired of this maze." I raised my paw to strike, and just then a bright light flickered on, making my eyes adjust. Just as I saw my target tailing it out of there, I heard what no cat wants to hear.

"Come on Emilita, it's time to go to sleep. What are you doing out here anyway? If we go now, I can comb you before bed!"

And in one fell swoop, my life of crime had landed me right back in the slammer.

Find out how The House became haunted.

Read *The Cabin*.


butwiththemind.com/cabin


enter the code:

nijia

# Acknowledgments

A huge thanks to the Newtown Historical Society for making so much of their rich history available online.

Thank you to my editor, Jeni Chappelle. You helped fix my comma key among other things.

Much appreciation to RiverRun Bookstore in Portsmouth, NH for the used, but useful ink ribbon on the cover.

Kerry, you've always got me covered. Thank you for taking whatever ideas I throw at you and making them art. LP4L.

Brittney, you've held the fate of my characters in your hands more than once. Thanks for listening to my late-night plot twists and always wanting to be the first to read whatever crazy thoughts come out of my head. That probably makes you crazy too.

Emilita, no one makes it more challenging to complete simple tasks, walk from one room to the next, or sleep at 4 *A.M.* You are perfect and I wouldn't have it any other way.

To Me, I wouldn't be where I am today, without you. And no, that's not a bad thing. Thank you.

# About the Author

Autumn Siders lives in New Hampshire with the world-famous cat, Emilita. She holds a Bachelor of Arts in English from the University of New Hampshire. She is the author of *#nofilter; Spermeo & Juliegg; She Loves Me, She Loves Me Not; Travels with Clancy;* and the E.M. Sanchez mysteries. She also poorly maintains the blog butwiththemind.com and is terrible at social media.